THEM

Look for other REMNANTS™ titles by K.A. Applegate:

#1 The Mayflower Project

#2 Destination Unknown

Also by K.A. Applegate

ANIMORPHS®

REMNANTS™

THEM

K.A. APPLEGATE

SCHOLASTIC INC.
New York Toronto London Auckland Sydney
Mexico City New Delhi Hong Kong Buenos Aires

For Michael and Jake

ISBN 0-590-88078-0

12 11 10 9 8 7 6 5 4 3 2 1 1 2 3 4 5 6 7/0

Printed in the U.S.A.
First Scholastic printing, November 2001

CHAPTER ONE

"HOW DOES BUGS BUNNY DO HALF THE STUFF HE DOES?"

They named the pony Eeyore.

He was a skanky-looking beast, shaggy and slumped over and hangdog. He was harnessed to a wagon that might fall apart at any moment. The big solid wheels creaked and wobbled. Neither pony nor cart would ever break three miles an hour. But they had managed to load the comatose Billy Weir into the back of the wagon.

They had food in the form of pies. Not fruit pies or cream pies, but meat pies, and the exact nature of the meat was anyone's guess. But it was food and they were hungry. They also had water. The water was in crockery jars that were no doubt supposed to contain mead or ale, but what did the ship know about any of that?

Jobs, Mo'Steel, Olga Gonzalez, who was Mo'Steel's mother, Violet Blake, who liked to be called Miss

Blake, and Billy Weir, who managed to be entirely catatonic and then, at unpredictable times, frighteningly powerful, were the most normal creatures in view. There were other humans all around, but not humans as they were in reality, humans as they had been imagined by a long-long-dead painter named Brueghel.

Pieter Brueghel the Elder had painted at about the same time that Nostradamus had written his prophecies, in the mid-1550s and early 1560s. That was, give or take, four-hundred-fifty years earlier than Jobs had been born, and not quite a thousand years earlier than the present moment.

Jobs was fourteen years old. Or five hundred and fourteen years old, depending on your perspective.

The Dutch painter could not have foreseen that his work would be inscribed on data disks that would find their way aboard a space shuttle called the *Mayflower* and from there end up being downloaded into an alien spaceship so vast it had at first seemed to be a planet.

Jobs and his companions were walking through a live-action version of an old painting. A live-action, 3-D, solid-to-the-touch, undeniably real version created by who or whatever was in charge of the alien ship.

"Why?" That was the question. And also "how?"

The improbable set of circumstances had begun with the destruction of Earth by an asteroid. Jobs and Mo'Steel had seen the impact from space. Earth was a watermelon dropped from the third floor. When last seen, Earth had been smacked into three big, irregular chunks flying apart in stately slo-mo.

But before that cosmic annihilation, humans had tried a desperate, last-minute, utterly doomed effort to save some tiny remnant of *Homo sapiens.* They had hauled a nearly antique shuttle out of storage, fitted it out with experimental solar sails and even more experimental hibernation equipment, and loaded up the so-called Mayflower Project with eighty humans chosen, according to time-honored ritual, from among those who had ties to, or influence over, NASA.

The *Mayflower* had no possibility of succeeding and indeed no one had expected it to. It had no destination, no goal. It had merely been fired into space, fired away from Earth.

And despite this it had been found far, far beyond the orbit of Neptune, out in cold empty space where good old Sol, Earth's sun, was just another twinkly star.

Found, recovered, picked up by the ship, by whoever or whatever ran the ship.

Those of the Eighty who had survived the moldy death called "cheesing," and death by mutated carnivorous worm, and death by micrometeorite, and death by mummification, had revived to find themselves in an environment created out of humanity's own creative patrimony. The ship had downloaded the *Mayflower*'s data and created an environment based on human art.

It must have seemed like a good idea to the ship. But at the moment, Jobs and his friends were walking beside a rickety pony-drawn cart through a gloomy landscape dominated by what was, according to Miss Blake, the Tower of Babel.

Brueghel's vision of the Tower of Babel, at least.

It looked a bit like a wedding cake. A wedding cake constructed of crumbling sports arenas piled one atop the other. A wedding cake done in the colors of old parchment and iced tea stains.

It was circular and there were layers, each one smaller in diameter than the one below. If construction had continued indefinitely it might have, in time, reached a sharp point. But construction had stopped at seven layers. It was a gigantic spiral ramp, and if construction had been sensibly completed it would have been possible to walk around and around the building and ascend to the top. But the Tower of Babel was a mess, with massive, tumbled-stone spurs defacing one side and blocking the rampway on at least three levels.

And toward the top of the tower it seemed the builders had changed their minds, cut away the outer layers, and begun construction on a tower-atop-a-tower, a sort of miniaturized, modest version of the tower rising from the tumbled wreckage of the original building. This mini-tower had the look of a castle's keep, or perhaps a sort of grandiose penthouse.

Each layer was penetrated by high-arched doors and windows, and the mini-tower likewise. The doors on lower levels were tall enough to allow a giraffe to walk through without ducking. Doors higher up were of more human dimensions.

The Tower of Babel fronted a harbor on one side. It had a low stone quay. The remaining three hundred degrees of arc was on land and loomed huge above a squalid, medieval city.

It was this city that Jobs was walking through, leading the pony. From this distance the tower was so tall, so vast in extent, so massively heavy that it seemed impossible that the ground could support it.

"Big," Mo'Steel remarked.

"I wonder how tall? If we had a stick, we could cut it to the length of my arm and figure it out," Jobs said. "All you have to do is hold the stick vertically and move back or closer till it appears to equal the height of the building. Then you just pace off —"

"Or we could just agree that it's really big," Violet Blake said.

Jobs knew her finger was bothering her. Her missing finger. The empty space where her tenth finger would have been. She unwound the bandage and Jobs looked away, squeamish.

The wound was still bleeding; it might go on bleeding forever. It was down to a slow seep now, a red ooze from beneath the cauterized crust and around the scab. It wasn't gushing at least. He winced just thinking about it.

"Strange how it doesn't just hurt at the knuckle where it was lopped off," Violet said through gritted teeth. "It hurts at the tip. I mean, the former tip. The no-longer-there tip."

"Phantom pain," Olga Gonzalez said sympathetically.

"You should change that bandage," Mo'Steel

said. He left the road and walked up to a peasant woman who was carrying a heavy bucket. "Excuse me, ma'am, I need your scarf."

Mo'Steel unwound the white cloth from the woman's head. The woman said nothing. In fact, she never slowed or stopped or responded. Beneath the scarf was blank space, no hair, no head, just emptiness. A second later a new scarf appeared, wrapped just like the one Mo'Steel had taken.

Mo'Steel handed the scarf to Violet. "Would you like me to help you with that?"

"No. No, thank you," she answered.

Mo'Steel caught up with Jobs. "I'd feel bad about taking stuff from these people, but they don't seem to mind."

"I don't think they mind anything," Jobs said. "I don't think they have minds. They're not real in the usual ways. They may not even be anatomically human, let alone have functioning wills."

Mo'Steel shrugged. "Maybe not."

"It never hurts to be polite," Olga, Mo'Steel's mother, opined.

"I was raised right," Mo'Steel said with a wink for Jobs and a sincere smile for his mother.

"The system conserves energy," Jobs said thoughtfully. "That's why when you take the scarf away there's nothing underneath. The system doesn't need to create matter to fill in beneath the scarf; it saves energy, it just does what it has to do. I'd bet some of these people don't weigh more than twenty pounds or so. You could pick them up and carry them. The system probably doesn't fill them in."

"They're three-dimensional illustrations," Miss Blake said.

Olga looked skeptical. "So how is it Eeyore can pull Billy? He shouldn't be strong enough if he's hollow."

"The strength doesn't come from muscles. It comes from the matter-manipulation system directly," Jobs said. He liked this sort of puzzle. It gave him a sense of satisfaction being able to construct a theory and defend it.

"They're like cartoons," Mo'Steel said. "Because they're drawings they can do stuff that doesn't make sense. I mean, how does Bugs Bunny do half the stuff he does?"

Jobs gave his friend a dirty look, which Mo'Steel reflected back as a gapped grin. Jobs knew when he was being teased.

"Why exactly are we heading for the tower?" Miss Blake demanded.

"It's tall. We climb it, maybe we'll be able to get

the lay of the land," Jobs said. "Besides, the others will head for it. Maybe we can hook up with them."

"Are you sure you want to?" Violet muttered.

Violet's mother, Wylson Lefkowitz-Blake, had taken charge of the Remnants. She was a dynamic, impressive woman. It had not escaped Jobs's notice that mother and daughter didn't get along at all.

"My brother's with them," Jobs pointed out. "Besides, strength in numbers and all that."

"Who do you think lives in the tower?" Olga wondered.

"More Cartoons," Jobs said with a shrug.

"Maybe they have a cartoon bath," Violet said wistfully. "A hot bath. With soap. And shampoo."

They turned a corner and suddenly there was no more town between them and the base of the tower. Jobs hauled back on Eeyore's bridle. They stood for a moment staring up at the structure, imposing and impossible and threatening.

"What was the story of the Tower of Babel? Does anyone know? It's a Bible thing, right?" Jobs asked.

Mo'Steel shook his head pityingly. "You are such a heathen, Duck. The people made a tower to reach all the way up to heaven. God didn't like their attitude, getting above themselves and all. So he turned them against one another by making them speak all different languages. That way they couldn't cooperate and make any more towers to heaven."

Jobs made a face. He was on the verge of saying that it was a stupid story. But Mo'Steel would be offended.

"An allegory of human pride," Miss Violet Blake said. "A pretty good allegory if you wish to instruct people in humility."

"But not as good as an asteroid," Jobs said dryly.

CHAPTER TWO

"YOU'RE REALLY JUMPY, YOU KNOW THAT?"

Yago liked the tower. No one else seemed to, but he did. One thing was for sure: If you wanted to be king you needed a castle. And this tower was the mother of all castles. It totally dominated the landscape, the biggest thing around by a factor of ten thousand percent or so.

The upper floors had possibilities, definitely. He could see setting up a throne room there. He would have the whole mini-tower to himself. All the lower floors would be for various servants, functionaries, soldiers, and so on.

Okay, it was a daydream, but what empire ever started without some crazy dream?

"I think we should see if we can make it a center of operations," Wylson Lefkowitz-Blake said, hands on hips. "Depending on whether it's already inhabited. I mean, it's pretty impressive, isn't it?"

Tamara Hoyle was standing stolidly with her creepy baby cantilevered out on one hip. Such a chubby baby, such a hard, bony, bodybuilder mother. They fascinated Yago. Why didn't the baby ever eat? How could it seem to see with those empty craters where its eyes had been? And surely it was too big to be natural. He was no expert on babies, but that was one freak of a baby. He edged away from Tamara and the baby, eased around to the other side of Wylson Lefkowitz-Blake. For the moment Wylson seemed to be running things. Which was fine with Yago: He would play the loyal number two for now.

"I think it would be perfect," Yago said. "I mean, look, the only way up is by following the spiral pathway, right? So couldn't you defend it with just a few people?"

The baby made a giggling sound and Tamara Hoyle snorted. "If we had five hundred troops, yes, you could hold it. But altitude and interior lines only go so far. How do you even know if someone is climbing the far side of the thing? It would take a hundred men just to monitor the perimeter."

"We need to be someplace," Wylson countered. "We need a corporate headquarters. A base of operations. I'd far rather be up there than down here.

If we can find a way to get some kind of radio system going, well, that's the highest point."

Yago looked away to hide his laugh. Radio? Corporate headquarters? Where did Wylson think she was? "Good thinking, boss."

The baby looked away, bored, and Tamara shrugged, indifferent.

Yago suppressed a shudder. He was right: In the end it would be the freaks against the normals. Tamara and the baby were the definition of freak. Them and Billy Weir, wherever he was, and of course, 2Face. He searched for and found her over by her father, Shy Hwang. Shy Hwang had a permanent mope glued onto his face, as though the death of his wife was a unique tragedy beside which the death of the entire human race paled to irrelevance. 2Face didn't seem as depressed, although who could tell with that half-melted face of hers? Hard to read her, though Yago had the definite impression that 2Face was a tough chick. Probably hot, too, back before her face was blowtorched. Half a nice face.

And she'd blown him off, that's what stuck. He'd tried to recruit her, back in the world, back in the before, he'd offered her the chance to be his first fan. He, Yago, universally hailed by every teen fanzine as the best-looking guy in America. He'd been *Teen*

People's Hunk of the Year two years in a row, unprecedented! Half the kids in the country had copied his spring-green hair and golden, cat's-DNA eyes.

And Candle Face had chilled him.

Yago bit his lip and tried to move past it. It was five hundred years ago, after all, and it wasn't like it mattered.

On the other hand, no one ever slammed Yago. He had dated Leonessa. He had dated Pet Proffer. Celebrities. Models.

Chilled by a freak? Yago?

He sensed D-Caf sidling up beside him. D-Caf was a natural toady, a born bootlicker. Plus he had not an ally in the place. He was a killer, he was, the little twitch. That didn't bother Yago. Much. A leader used the human material he was given.

"Are we going up there?" D-Caf asked.

"What do you care?" Yago asked.

D-Caf shrugged. "I was just wondering. It's kind of creepy, isn't it? I mean, I don't know, it's just creepy. Isn't there somewhere else we can go?"

"You're really jumpy, you know that?" Yago said.

D-Caf grinned and ducked his head. "I guess I am."

"Here's what you do: Don't worry about where we go. Just do what I tell you."

D-Caf frowned and looked uncertain.

Yago drew him closer, leaning in for a false confidentiality. "Your job is to watch 2Face. See, I think maybe she's a problem. So you keep an eye on her, and you tell me if she does anything."

"Like what?"

"Just keep an eye on her, okay, Twitch?"

D-Caf nodded. Yago slapped him on the back. "Good deal. Now get lost."

Wylson said, "Yago, tell everyone we're going."

"Everyone" consisted of Wylson and Yago as leaders; 2Face and her father, Shy Hwang, and her temporary ward, Edward, as likely enemies; Tamara and the baby, just out-and-out freaks; D-Caf, who was already halfway coopted; and then some unknowns: a kid named Roger Dodger who couldn't be much over ten, a kind of tough-looking chick named Tate, and a sixteen-year-old beast of a guy named Anamull, who looked like he might be of some use as an enforcer; finally, the two other adults, Daniel Burroway, who was some kind of scientist, and T.R., who was a shrink. Of the two, Burroway might be trouble someday, but T.R. was a worm.

Yago made a mental note: Work on Anamull. Muscle was always helpful. As Anamull was demonstrating. He had cornered one of the automaton people, one of the fake creatures who inhabited this weird artscape, and was busy stealing the man's dagger.

Not a bad idea, Yago thought. They should acquire whatever weapons they could, while they could. Who knew what was up in that tower?

"Anamull," Yago yelled. "As soon as you get that knife, let's go. Tate? Shy? Let's go, boys and girls."

"Where are we going?" Tate demanded.

Yago jerked a thumb. "Up there. Saddle up or be left behind. Where's that kid, Roger?"

Just then he spotted Roger Dodger. The kid was a block away, down the disjointed street. He was running and yelling.

Yago assumed he'd gotten into some trouble with one of the automatons. Which was strange, because the "locals" never objected to anything you did. They weren't really humans.

Yago strained to hear what Roger was shouting.

"Riders!" Tate translated. "He says Riders are coming!"

CHAPTER THREE

"I'M THE PRESIDENT'S SON, YOU KNOW."

Yago froze. What? Here?

"Wylson!" he cried. "Riders! Riders!"

That got everyone moving. They formed into a mass and the mass started stampeding. Through the narrow, pig-dropping-dotted streets, tripping over uneven cobblestones, careening off indifferent locals.

They ran, with Wylson, like any good leader, out in front. Yago had to admire the fact that her muscles, acquired during daily workouts with a personal trainer, had survived five centuries of hibernation. She was strong.

Yago glanced back over his shoulder but he couldn't see anything. At least nothing but Roger Dodger, steadily gaining.

A cart pulled out of a side alley. Piled high with hay, a moving haystack. Yago jerked left and jumped the yoke. He caught his foot and went sprawling. Elbows on cobblestones and a sharp jolt of pain. Then he was up, scrambling, Roger Dodger even with him now.

He was falling behind! He was in the rear! They were going to leave him for the Riders. No way, no way he couldn't outrun Shy Hwang, who was a wheezy chub.

Then it occurred to Yago: He'd taken a wrong turn. He'd lost them! He couldn't see anyone but Roger Dodger.

"Hey, kid! Hey, kid!" he yelled. No answer, no look. The kid was a rabbit.

Had to head for the tower, no other way, no other way, but where was the tower? Ahead? Left? To the right? How had he gotten so turned around?

Yago bolted down an alley, even filthier than the street, even more narrow, with the buildings leaning drunkenly out till their upper stories almost touched.

A sudden, looming horror, straight ahead.

Rider!

Coming straight down the street. He was atop his surfboard, shifting his weight minutely to keep the antigravity board from striking the walls on either side.

Yago took in the bifurcated legs, the cockroach-shell upper body, and most of all the two heads, fraternal not identical twins, one little more than a mouth on a stump, and the other dominated by six spider eyes. He squeezed his legs together to keep from wetting himself, spun, and ran.

The Rider couldn't move at top speed in the alley, but he could still outrun Yago.

Yago was screaming as he ran and the Rider let loose with his horrifying, metal-on-metal shriek. Yago almost collapsed right then, but the memory of Errol's disconnected head kept him running.

Where were the others? Where was that kid? Let the Rider take the kid! Why didn't the alien eat the automatons? How did he know that Yago was food and the locals weren't?

Glance.

Ten feet!

Slam. Into one of the locals, tumble, fall, roll, and look up as the Rider skimmed overhead, unable to stop in time. The Rider braked, spun his board, eyeballed Yago with his larger faceted eyes, grinned with his vicious mouth.

Yago whimpered, rolled, kicked himself up, stumbled and fell, up again, crying, no no no no.

A side alley. Even more narrow. Narrow enough?

Yago lurched, tripped. The Rider turned, stopped,

couldn't go any closer. Yago was on his butt, kicking, sliding backward away from the Rider. The alley was too narrow! Too narrow for the Rider's board.

"Yeah!" Yago yelled triumphantly.

Then the Rider jumped down off his board.

The Rider bounded toward Yago, a weird stride, two feet on either side, or else two legs on either side, hard to define which. The Rider bounded and stopped, gathered strength, bounded again.

Yago was already running but he was encouraged that at least the Riders weren't all that fast on foot. The Rider hesitated with each jump. A ten-foot leap, a five-second pause, a ten-foot leap, five-second pause. The distance between Yago and the Rider kept going from fifteen feet to five feet and back.

Yago wasn't gaining but he wasn't losing ground, either.

He staggered into a woman carrying a large clay pot on her head. The pot went flying, smashed to bits.

Yago kept running, out into an open space. Not quite a square, but at least a place where a maze of streets joined from all angles. Which way? The tower! He could see it.

The Rider had stopped. Maybe he was worn out. Then Yago spotted the hoverboard. It was flying just above the rooftops and now swooped down to rejoin its master.

"No fair!" Yago yelled.

He ran for a doorway, open for a man who was exiting. He shoved past the automaton and stopped dead. There was nothing inside the building. Just open space. The building was a shell.

Yago blinked.

Suddenly the building had an inside. It had an inside filled with soft, golden candlelight, ornate, plush furniture, and a woman reclining on a brocaded couch. A painting in 3-D. It even looked familiar.

"What?" Yago wondered.

The ship was improvising. The ship had seen him go into the building, and, having no obvious interior scene to construct, it had grabbed one from some other file.

"Excuse me," Yago said to the indifferent, unreal woman. He ran up the stairs. Up another floor. Another interior, gloomy this time, but with a huge window at one end of the room. The window was open.

Yago crept to the window, trembling, jittery, wanting to throw up but too scared of the noise it would make.

He peered out at the street below. Left. Right. No Rider.

Then, coming down the street, Wylson Lefkowitz-Blake and the rest of the bunch.

"Hey!" Yago yelled. "Hey, I'm up here!"

Wylson frowned. "What are you doing up there?"

"I was chased here by a Rider."

"We assumed he'd gotten you," Wylson said without revealing any particular concern.

"No, I'm still alive," Yago snapped.

"Then you'd better come down. The Riders must still be around. We need to get to the tower."

"Yeah, and it sure is good to know you survived, Yago," Yago said, but under his breath. "Thank god you made it, Yago."

The Wylson woman just didn't get it: He was important. Yago was not one of the herd. He was important.

He glanced at the reclining woman on the couch as he passed by.

"I'm the president's son, you know." He pointed at himself. "Yago. That's me."

CHAPTER FOUR

"I HATE THIS PLACE."

Jobs had seen no Riders. At one point he'd been sure he heard someone yell, "No fair!" which seemed like an unlikely thing to come from the mouth of one of the automatons — or Cartoons as Mo'Steel called them.

He no longer entirely trusted his senses. They had reached the base of the tower and found steep walls and no easy way up. But there was the strange stone abutment that ran the height of three levels. It looked as if the tower had been carved from living rock and this jagged outcropping was all that was left of what had to have been a mountain.

It was steep, a hard climb, especially now that they'd had to say good-bye to Eeyore and transfer Billy back to his stretcher.

The climb would have been impossible but for

the fact that Mo'Steel was quite strong and hauled Billy up almost single-handedly over the roughest parts.

It was perhaps a two-hundred- or two-hundred-and-fifty-foot climb and in places was like crawling up a cliff. At the top Mo'Steel sweated and grinned and gave Jobs a last yank up and over.

"That was good," Mo'Steel said, wiping his brow. "Drain the pores, strain some muscle, pop some veins. Burning the C's."

Jobs looked at Billy. His gaunt, pale face showed nothing new. The shadowed eyes continued to stare.

Olga flopped down, tired. Violet Blake took a moment to find a tumbled rock to sit on. Her skirt was frayed at the hem. Her frilled sleeves were stained with blood and sweat.

All in all, Jobs thought, the whole ultrafeminine "Jane" look really didn't work for rock climbing. Besides, she was a very pretty girl, especially now that she'd given up on keeping her long, sandy hair tied up. It looked better down over her shoulders.

Violet Blake saw his smug look. She carefully folded her hands in her lap and favored him with a defiant smile.

Jobs looked down, not wanting his admiring grin

to be misinterpreted as condescension. Then he scanned the horizon. He was looking back over the direction from which they'd come. At the far range of his vision he saw the sight that stabbed at his heart: the shuttle, a white stiletto, far away now. He looked long, storing up the image for later. It was worth a poem. Someday, somewhere, maybe.

"Should have stayed with the shuttle," he muttered. "It was home."

Mo'Steel overheard and slapped him on the back. "Don't sweat it, Duck. We'll make a new home."

Jobs didn't want to be jollied out of his mood. He was tired and he wanted for the moment just to savor the melancholy. There was nothing wrong with sadness. Sadness was a good emotion. It was a tribute to all that had been lost: to family, to friends, to the billions of people, long dead now, who were only family in the sense that they shared human DNA.

A planet destroyed, a million species obliterated, the human race reduced to these Remnants, lost, that was worth some sadness.

"It's been five hundred years," Jobs whispered.

"Not to us," Miss Blake said. "To us it was only days ago."

"Hey, look," Olga said. She stood up and pointed. "It's the others."

They could be clearly seen, a gaggle of people in colors too bright and with too many blond heads to be Brueghel Cartoons. They were at the edge of the town below, and they were running toward the tower.

"Riders!" Mo'Steel yelled and jumped to his feet.

Three of the rust-red aliens were pursuing. Two more were coming in from an angle, racing to cut them off.

"We have to help them," Miss Blake said.

"It took us an hour to climb up here," Olga said. "It would take almost as long to get back down, and then we'd have to traverse over to them."

The four of them stood at the edge of the drop, staring, eyes bulging, straining as if straining would slow the Riders down or lend speed to the rest of the group.

One of the fugitives was smaller, slight, and moved with the slight ungainliness of a child. The wispy, almost translucent blond hair could be clearly seen.

"I see Edward," Jobs said grimly.

The running, panic-stricken crowd was hidden

from view by the tower itself. Four sighs, four worried looks.

"Maybe they can find a place to hide," Violet said.

Jobs nodded, silent. He was sick with worry. His parents were gone. He was all Edward had in the world. His little brother was his responsibility now, and Jobs wasn't down there but up here. He should have tried harder to find the others and get back together. Should have done something.

He squeezed his eyes shut tight trying to keep out the image of Edward being taken, killed by the Riders.

"I hate this place," Violet said with sudden passion. "Why is it this way? Why go to all the trouble of creating these environments and then let those alien murderers run rampant? Is this stupid place trying to save us or kill us?"

Jobs shook his head. "Maybe neither." He rubbed the heels of his hands into his eyes. "Maybe the ship isn't all that in control. Look at how the Blue Meanies got in. How can whoever or whatever is running this ship have all this power and then be unable to stop the Blue Meanies?"

"You always say whoever or *whatever,* Jobs," Olga said. "You know something we don't?"

"No." He was about to add that he had a feeling, an instinct. But he had nothing to go on. And in any case, it was too easy to talk about abstractions. His brother was down there somewhere, without a mother or a father or a soul in the world to help him, down there facing the ruthless, murdering savages called Riders. That's what he should be thinking about.

He glared at Billy. "Can't you do something? I know you can hear me. We know you're not dead, Billy. We saw you floating around in the air and trying to help your dad when you had to, when he was screaming — why can't you do that now?"

No response, not even a flicker.

"I *hate* this place," Violet repeated savagely.

Jobs wanted to agree. This place was probably killing his brother, right now, right this second. But he didn't hate it. He couldn't. Not till he knew for sure what it was.

CHAPTER FIVE

"EVERYTHING DIES, HUMAN."

"Get in! Get in! Get in!" Wylson yelled.

They got in. They ran like a herd of gazelles with a lion hot on the trail.

Into the dark-on-dark archway, into the tower.

No door, Wylson thought. *No way to block the Riders. Was everyone in? Had everyone made it? 2Face, Shy, Burroway, T.R., Roger Dodger. Who else? No time to worry.*

A glance around. Where were they? A vaulted chamber, nothing around but space, an echoing space like a gothic cathedral, high-arched space. Keep them running, that was all.

"Keep moving, keep moving," she shouted. Her voice was shrill, she hated that, it was the fear.

They kept running, but where? A Rider appeared, a shadow in the archway.

"Stairs!" someone yelled.

"Go!" Wylson cried.

The Rider was moving cautiously, unsure of himself in this interior environment. The hoverboard inched forward. What Wylson thought of as the creature's "spider head" craned, back and forth, upward. The alien almost seemed to cringe.

Doesn't like it, Wylson thought. *Doesn't like being enclosed. Or maybe it's the dark.* A second Rider joined the first.

The people were on the stairs now, narrow, hacked from stone, a sheer drop if you strayed, no handrail.

Someone tripped and those behind plowed into and over him. It was the kid, Edward. People were always bumping into him, clumsy brat.

2Face snatched at the kid's collar and yanked him after her. Up and up and Wylson glanced back to see that three Riders had entered the chamber, huddling together, uncertain.

Then, one of them hefted a spear and threw it with shocking speed. It missed T.R.'s head by a whisker and jammed hard into the stone wall.

Wylson reached the spot and tried to yank the spear out. She didn't have the strength. Tamara Hoyle grabbed the shaft and pulled. It came free.

The baby chuckled and Tamara handed the spear to Wylson with a mocking little bow.

Wylson nodded and took the steps two at a time, holding the spear high like a prize. When she glanced back she saw the three Riders apparently still undecided. Then she noticed Tamara. The Marine sergeant was standing, facing the Riders, the baby on one hip, a fist propped on the other.

"Tamara! Don't be stupid!" Wylson yelled.

Tamara showed no sign of having heard her. The three aliens were now focused entirely on the woman and child. One hefted a spear, hesitated.

Tamara made a little gesture with her free hand. Bring it on.

The alien snarled and threw. Tamara moved with liquid grace, dodged, and snatched the spear out of the air.

The Riders gave her a cold look. A mean look, with one head staring and the other gnashing its razor teeth.

One of the Riders urged his hoverboard forward. It flowed easily up the first dozen stairs, but then it slowed and seemed to be straining to keep climbing.

Tamara Hoyle waited, confident. She sat the baby

down on a stair. It was the first time Wylson had ever seen them separated.

"What are you doing? They'll kill you!" Wylson shouted.

But Tamara was indifferent. She kept going toward the Rider, taking the steps with feline grace, with a feline's air of power-within-grace.

The Rider let loose its glass-shattering shriek. Tamara replied with a feral laugh. Sitting on the edge of its stone step the baby clapped its hands.

Tamara was now almost face-to-face with the alien. The hoverboard quivered, unable to climb farther. In a rush, the alien leaped onto the stairs. It swung a bladed weapon like a scimitar.

Tamara caught the blow with her spear, twisted the spear, threw the Rider off-balance, and stabbed the spear into one if its heads.

The alien shrieked again but in a very different tone.

Tamara pulled back, spun her entire body, and slapped the alien's other head with the butt of the spear. With blinding speed she jabbed the butt into one of the larger fly eyes.

The Rider swung his scimitar again, but Tamara easily ducked the blow and buried the point of her spear in the Rider's chest, in a narrow gap between halves of its beetle armor.

The Rider staggered, fell back onto its hoverboard.

The hoverboard clattered down the stairs, as lifeless as the Rider.

Tamara ignored her kill and stared instead at the two remaining Riders.

To Wylson's amazement, the two aliens executed what could only be a salute, a sort of half-genuflection in the direction of the Marine sergeant.

No, not to Tamara. They were bowing to the baby.

One of the Riders turned and flew away. The other stayed behind, waiting, not trying to ascend the stairs. But not giving way, either.

Tamara retrieved the baby and came up the stairs, spear shouldered, unconcerned by the purple blood oozing down its length.

"You killed it," Wylson said stupidly.

"Did you think they were immortal?" Tamara said. "Everything dies, human."

CHAPTER SIX

"I THINK WE NEED TO HAVE A MEETING."

Wylson ran up the stairs, up to rejoin the others who had already moved ahead.

Some of them had seen the fight. Had any of them heard the Marine's last remark?

"Everything dies, human."

Had she heard it right? Everything dies, human? Everything human dies? Everything dies that's human?

Tamara was stressed from the combat. The words came out wrong, that was all. *Not a time to start going soft-headed, Wylson,* she told herself. *Time to focus on solutions.*

The stairs arrived at the next floor. It was brighter here, though still gloomy. 2Face and Roger Dodger had fanned out to check the limits of the room.

"No way out," 2Face yelled at Wylson when she appeared. "Except for that way." She indicated the high, arched doorway that led outside.

Wylson stuck her head out of the arch. It opened onto the spiral path that circled the tower. To the right, downhill, uphill was left. She craned her head up, nothing but blank, yellowed stone wall above.

The path was perhaps thirty feet across at this point. Equally far to the left and right were arched doors superficially similar to the one she was in.

"There's a door over here," Roger Dodger yelled from back inside.

Wylson pulled her head in. She still held her own spear awkwardly, across her chest. She'd done nothing with it to help Tamara.

Tamara twirled her purple-blooded spear with unconscious ease and lounged by the top of the stairs as if waiting for the remaining Rider to come up after her.

Wylson went to where a crowd had gathered around Roger Dodger. There was a door there, too short, too small. It was wood bound with iron.

"Should we open it?" Burroway wondered aloud.

Wylson was on the verge of saying yes, but there was something about the door. Something that made her insides twist.

"Alice in Wonderland," Tate said. She shrugged. "Maybe there's a garden on the other side."

"I don't think so," Wylson said. But it bothered her, not being able to pinpoint a reason. When the *Wall Street Journal* had done their big feature on her company, they had described Wylson Lefkowitz-Blake as a CEO who could demand the most meticulous research and yet still decide to "go with her gut."

It had been a great piece. A high point in her life, along with getting the cover of *BusinessWeek*, and of course the first couple of days when her personal wealth had gone from less than a million to better than fourteen million.

What was she worth now? More than a billion.

A billion dollars issued by a government that no longer existed on a dead planet.

Wylson had always trusted her instincts and her instincts said not to open that door. But these weren't her business instincts, these were something else from somewhere else deep in her brain. This was a voice she'd never heard in her head, a shivering, pleading voice.

Don't open the door.

Don't open the door.

They were all looking at her. Looking at her and glancing back to the stair where Tamara and the baby stood guard.

All waiting for her to decide.

"Well, open it," she said impatiently.

Anamull, the big kid, the sixteen-year-old who looked like he should be playing for the NFL, grinned and grabbed the wrought-iron latch. He pulled. Nothing. He pulled harder and the door opened.

Inside squatted a creature with a woman's face, a white scarf, a red dress, and legs and feet that must have belonged to a frog. The woman held a long-handled iron pan over a charcoal fire.

In the pan was a human head, hand, leg. The head was screaming in agony.

Behind the woman stood an antlered deer, standing on its hind legs, wearing a robe. The deer just stared at them.

Wylson cried out, jumped back. Anamull wailed and slammed the door shut. It bounced open. 2Face slammed it again and this time Anamull leaned his weight into it and the door stayed closed.

"What was that?" Burroway demanded, his voice quaking.

"Not a garden," 2Face said, breathing heavily.

Wylson was trembling. What was that, what, what? She swallowed hard. Some kind of trick. Some kind of illusion. Not real. Obviously.

Her insides had gone liquid. The vision — illusion, surely, special effect — had turned reality inside out for a moment.

Shake it off.

She pried her hands apart, couldn't look like she was scared. She was in charge.

"We're trapped in here," Shy Hwang said. "Can't go back down the stairs, sure can't go through that door."

"There's the path outside," Wylson said, recovering enough now to take offense at Shy's despairing tone. One thing was sure: His daughter had all the spine in that family.

Yago said, "You go right on that ramp path, it takes you back down to the town. You go left, it takes you up. Except we don't know that for sure because you could see that the tower was damaged."

"Sergeant? Are the Riders still down there at the bottom of the stairs?" Daniel Burroway demanded.

"Only one," Tamara answered. "I killed one. One took off."

"Why?" Wylson wondered aloud. "I mean, why did one take off?"

"Why do you think?" Tamara replied sardonically. "They don't like the stairs. I don't think their boards can do stairs very well. So they're looking for another way."

"Up the ramp," Yago said. "They'll come right up the ramp."

The baby nodded, eager, excited. His mother smiled.

"You killed one of them?" 2Face demanded skeptically.

"She did," Wylson confirmed. Feeling she needed to add an explanation, she said, "She's a professional soldier, after all. Trained with weapons." The explanation reassured her. That's all it was: Tamara Hoyle was a Marine sergeant. Of course she'd be able to fight. Nothing unnatural in that.

"We have two spears and one 'professional soldier,'" Burroway said darkly. "If the Riders come after us in force, up that ramp, we can't hope to stop them."

"Thank you, Mr. Happy," Yago muttered. "Hey, we'll just put the freak here in the doorway — that'll scare them off." He jerked a thumb at 2Face. "Put Half 'n' Half here, and the baby out there, hey, that'd scare anyone. What's the point of having freaks if we can't use them?"

Wylson shot a look at Tamara to see if she'd taken offense. Tamara seemed bored.

2Face's face was turning dark, at least the normal side of her face.

"Hey, did you see those Riders? They're so ugly even *she* couldn't scare them," Anamull added.

Wylson knew she should shut Yago up; he was sowing discord. But however crude and cruel he might be, Yago was on her side. *Besides,* Wylson told herself, *she was the boss, not some kind of preschool teacher promoting good behavior.*

2Face looked as if she could take care of herself, after all; her own father hadn't exactly jumped in to defend her. And anyway, she surely could have had plastic surgery. She didn't have to look that way.

What am I supposed to do? Wylson asked herself. *The boss has to know. The boss has to be in charge. Unless . . .*

"I think we need to have a meeting," Wylson said, trying to sound decisive. "T.R., Burroway, Shy, Tamara, if you . . . and Yago, you, too, to speak for the younger people. Meeting in five minutes: We need ideas, people." She clapped her hands together sharply.

That was the right thing: a meeting of senior staff.

Get organized. Set priorities. Assign tasks.

She was the woman who had taken on AvivNet and Microsoft and SpongeCom and won. She could do this.

Of course, a suppressed part of her mind commented, this really was worse. Business competitors didn't decapitate their victims and suck the flesh from their skulls. Or fry people in cast-iron pans.

Not even Microsoft.

CHAPTER SEVEN

"AN ALL-OVER SQUIRM."

"This is new damage." Jobs pointed at the crushed rock, then at the long burn scar.

Mo'Steel watched his friend closely. He could see that Jobs was scared for Edward. Maybe for himself as well. That was a surprising thought. Mo'Steel thought of Jobs as fearless, but now that he considered it, that didn't seem quite right.

"Yeah, it looks like it just happened," Mo'Steel agreed. They had come to a rest, having circumnavigated about half of the tower. This side of the tower was much more regular in appearance. Miss Blake had explained that they were now on the side that was not shown in the original painting.

"The ship is extrapolating," Jobs said.

Mo'Steel was fairly sure he knew what Jobs meant but the word *extrapolating* was not one he used. Anyway, the idea seemed to be that the ship was filling in the blanks in the original painting.

"At least that proves whoever is doing all this has an imagination," Olga said.

"Not necessarily," Jobs argued. "The continuation of a pattern doesn't imply imagination. Program a computer with a grid, it can figure out how to extend the grid."

Violet sighed. Mo'Steel had noticed that she had no patience for Jobs's explanations. And she showed no particular interest now as Jobs walked deeper into the arched opening, following the scorch mark.

Jobs pressed his hand against the stone. "It's still warm."

Mo'Steel put his hand on Jobs's shoulder. "We don't want to be going in there any farther."

"Why not?"

"It's dark."

"Not yet it isn't," Jobs said.

Mo'Steel shook his head. "You don't get a wiggle off this place?"

"A what?"

Mo'Steel pointed at his own stomach. "A wiggle worm in the guts, 'migo. A bad feeling. An all-over squirm."

Jobs shrugged. "It's an environment derived from a painting. A creepy painting. That's all. Some artist was going for a look. That doesn't make it anything real."

Mo'Steel shrugged and felt a little foolish. Of course Jobs was right.

"Besides, maybe there's an interior ramp. It would have to be easier than walking the circumference of this whole tower, right?"

"Yeah, well, then we all go together. I'm not leaving my mom back there."

Jobs nodded. "Of course. Let's just go in a ways, see what we see. We can always back out."

They returned to gather Olga and Violet and to lift Billy once more.

They entered through the arch, talking animatedly all the while to ward off the sense of being too small for their surroundings. The place had an echoing hush to it, a feeling Mo'Steel associated with class trips to the State House in Sacramento.

The room was huge, but finite. There was a pointed archway at the far end, narrower, taller, sharper than the archway they'd entered through.

They peeked through this new arch and found the space beyond no darker, despite the fact that the weak sunlight was far away now.

"Look at this." Jobs pointed down at the floor. There was a dark smudge, like someone had dragged charcoal. Jobs frowned and moved off to the right, leaving Billy behind.

"It hit here!" he yelled.

Mo'Steel joined him.

"See? So whatever it was, it came flying in through the arch, scraping the wall the whole way, burning, slammed into this wall, fell. Then dragged itself through the pointy arch."

"Why are you talking like you knew what it was?" Mo'Steel demanded.

"Because I think I do know. I think it was a Blue Meanie. They came this way, we know that. Some of them were damaged. Maybe one crashed here."

"So why aren't we going the other way, outta here?" Mo'Steel asked.

Jobs grinned. "Mo, man, these Blue Meanies haven't done us any harm. And one thing's for sure: They know more than we do about what's going on."

"Uh-huh. Let's keep going, then." The bad feeling had not gone away. Didn't Jobs feel it, too? Maybe not. Jobs could feel when a computer program was wrong. Maybe that ability obscured the more primitive ability to sense danger.

"Shh!" Jobs held up a finger.

Everyone froze and listened. A distinct sound of movement, of heavy steps, irregular, syncopated. Like a horse's walk, maybe.

Mo'Steel handed his half of Billy's stretcher to his mother and moved out front. His mom gave him a "be careful" look and he winked back.

They had reached the end of the second empty, echoing chamber. Another doorway, not an archway this time, just a big rectangular doorway.

Mo'Steel poked his head through and motioned everyone else to stay back. The room beyond was roughly circular, with two sets of steps climbing the walls, and dark holes where other stairs must be heading down.

And there, turned to face them, waiting at bay, charred and banged up but still alive, was a Blue Meanie.

"Hi," Mo'Steel said.

CHAPTER EIGHT

"IS HE SOME KIND OF MUTANT?"

This would probably be a great opportunity, Yago thought. *Except for the very real possibility of getting killed.*

Wylson knew nothing about fighting a battle. She was out of her depth. Lost, confused, and afraid, and trying unsuccessfully to hide it.

This was the moment when a real leader like Yago could seize the moment. Only he had no idea what to do, either.

They had two spears. Anamull had his dagger. The Riders were likely to appear at any moment. And for the last forty-five minutes Wylson had been conducting a staff meeting that involved the adults plus Yago squatting in a corner, equally far from the arch, the stairs, and the tiny door to hell.

Most of the ideas they came up with had to do with organization. Wylson wanted departments with department heads. Burroway kept talking about a more military structure: platoons. T.R. favored a less hierarchical structure. Shy Hwang said nothing, just maintained his distant silence punctuated by grief-stricken sighs.

Tamara Hoyle and the baby were ignored since she'd refused to join the meeting. But Tamara was the point as far as Yago could see. They had one fighter: Tamara. They had one asset: Tamara. Wylson had told them all how the Marine had dispatched the Rider.

The meeting was going nowhere in increasingly desperate circles. Time for Yago to offer his own ideas.

"The first thing we need to do," he said, "is to make sure we're all on the same team."

"Obviously we are," T.R. said.

"No," Yago said. "You think the teams are human versus alien. My question is, how can we be sure some of us aren't really some of *them*? You going to tell me the baby is a regular old baby? You can't win a war when you have to watch your back."

"This isn't the time," Burroway said impatiently.

"Why can't we at least ask Tamara what's going on?" Yago asked reasonably. "Don't we have a right to know what side she's on? Her and 2Face, both."

Yago watched their faces and refused to let a smile of triumph appear on his own lips. So easy. It was a lesson he'd learned in his mother's White House: When people can't figure out how to come to grips with a hard thing, give them an easy thing to do.

Wylson looked thoughtfully at Tamara. "We do have a right to know what she's about. Her and the baby."

"And 2Face and Edward," Yago added. "The issue here is who is with us and who is against us."

"There's no reason to doubt 2Face," Burroway grumbled.

"Quit picking on my daughter," Shy Hwang said. "You hate her because her face is burned. You're a sick person, Yago."

"There's nothing wrong with 2Face," Wylson pronounced with finality.

"Really?" Yago waited till he had everyone's attention. Then he nodded toward 2Face and Edward. "Look at the kid. Edward. Watch him closely and you'll see it."

They watched. Stared. Edward was amusing himself, jumping over cracks between the paving stones. His clothing was torn and tattered like everyone's, but his seemed to match the color of the walls. He passed in front of the small door. And for just a flicker of time he seemed to be part of the door. Then he was past it and his face and arms and clothing all resumed a coloration similar to that of the stone.

"What was that?" T.R. demanded.

Yago said, "He's been doing it for a while now. It's subtle so you don't notice unless you look right at him, and since he's so quiet mostly no one looks. He's some kind of chameleon. Now that you've noticed . . . but you know who would have noticed a long time ago? Who's been taking care of Edward? 2Face has."

In fact, Yago hadn't noticed, either. It was the Twitch, D-Caf, who had pointed it out.

"Is he some kind of mutant?" Wylson demanded.

"And maybe not the only one," Yago said in a low voice. "Tamara and the baby, Edward, and probably 2Face since she's been covering up for Edward. Like I said: We have to know who is with us, and who isn't really even like us."

"I'm not listening to any more of this," Shy said and shuffled away. He didn't go straight to his daughter, but Yago knew he would soon enough.

Fine, let him report back to 2Face. Let her make

her move. Yago had things well in hand. Unless the Riders came and killed them all. In which case political game-playing wouldn't matter very much.

Have to stay focused on the future, Yago told himself. Maybe the Riders would come and kill them all. But maybe they wouldn't. And in that case Yago had laid the foundation for his own rise to power.

Sure enough, Hwang was sidling over toward his daughter. And she was turning her good ear to hear him. She stared daggers across the room at Yago. Yago made a little kissy-mouth at her and then laughed.

Tamara suddenly stood up, baby on her hip, and sauntered to the arch. It was growing dark outside. She seemed to be listening, and while she did, everyone watched.

The baby made its obscene little chuckle.

"Pretty soon," Tamara remarked laconically. "Pretty soon, and a lot of them."

CHAPTER NINE

"WE COME IN PEACE?"

The Blue Meanie stared. Waited.

He was smaller than a horse, maybe pony-size. Four legs without evident feet. Powerpuff Girl legs. Two serpentine tentacles, one on each side of his low-slung grazer's head.

He might have been made out of liquid night, so black that he was blue only where light touched him directly. He had eyes, one on each side, again like a horse, but there was no life in those eyes, no sign of a soul burning through.

Jobs was probably right: *It was a suit of some sort,* Violet thought. *Something was alive inside it, something presumably more vulnerable than this frightening apparition.*

One tentacle seemed to have been chopped in half. The midnight armor was scarred and scraped. The rocket-powered hind legs moved stiffly; both were charred black. The Meanie had definitely experienced some trouble. But he didn't look as bad as he should, for slamming into a stone wall.

The creature waved its tentacles in quick, intricate patterns. Maybe some kind of language, communication. But when none of the humans responded in kind it stopped and simply waited.

"Go ahead," Mo'Steel urged Jobs. "Talk to it."

"I don't know what to say," Jobs admitted.

"We come in peace?" Olga suggested.

"Actually, we do," Jobs said.

Violet took a step forward. "He may recognize that I'm female. Maybe that will reassure him." That was her stated reason for taking the lead. The real reason was that she felt she wasn't carrying her part of the burden. With her finger she couldn't carry the stretcher, and that had meant the two boys had done most of the work. Violet was perfectly content with the notion that men and women had different abilities, different duties, and different avocations. But she wasn't content being a burden. She had to contribute something beyond her ability to recognize the artistic antecedents of the environments.

Besides, she didn't feel that the Meanie was threatening. It was wary, yes. But it wasn't interested in killing her.

"Hello. I'm Miss Blake. Violet Blake." She pointed slowly to herself and repeated, "Miss Blake. I'm very pleased to make your acquaintance."

The Meanie watched with its soulless eyes.

She pointed at Jobs and said his name, at Mo'Steel and Olga, saying each name in turn. Then at Billy Weir.

She held her hands open, the universal sign (she hoped) that she carried no weapon and meant no harm.

The Meanie stared.

"Hey," Jobs said.

"What?" Violet snapped, frustrated by the alien's total lack of response.

"It's Billy," Jobs said.

Violet stepped back two steps, turned, hoping this wasn't some sort of culturally offensive move, and looked at Billy Weir.

His eyes were closed. His mouth was moving. Like slow, slow speech.

From the corner of her eye, Violet caught movement. The Blue Meanie. It rose slowly, standing awkwardly on its hind legs. This revealed a flat oval panel on the front of its suit, on its chest, assuming always it had a chest.

Violet looked from Billy to the alien. There was

no beam of light between them, nothing anyone could see, but something was happening.

And then, looking past Billy, through the rectangular door, through the distant peaked archway beyond, through the nearly forgotten arch that led outside, Violet saw something that brought her heart to her throat.

In a blaze of orange and red, the far-off sun was setting.

Darkness obliterated the outer door. Night had fallen. The darkness did not deepen inside the tower, but night was felt nevertheless.

From all around now, from every shadowed corner, came sounds of shuffling, movement, dragging, and now malevolent whispering and sharp, hysterical tittering laughter that rose to a shriek.

"What the . . ." Olga cried.

"Someone's there," Jobs hissed.

Filling the rectangular doorway and cutting off any escape, standing on the steps, edging into the room, came every nightmare of a brilliant, twisted, poisoned mind.

Demons and monsters.

"Last Judgment," Violet whispered.

CHAPTER TEN

"BOSCH."

"Ya-ahh!" Jobs cried.

"Whoa!" Mo'Steel yelled.

The demons skittered into the room, circling, keeping their distance but getting closer all the while.

"Bosch," Violet said. "Oh, lord. It's Bosch."

An antlered deer stood on its hind legs and stared at her.

Across the floor moved a huge fish head. The fish head had two human legs attached. The legs wore black boots and propelled the monster with kicks and scuffs. Protruding from the fish's gaping mouth was the lower half of a human torso. The fish seemed to be trying to finish the human meal, kicking with its booted feet, trying to swallow more.

A huge rat walked erect and wore a Tin Man funnel hat.

A monstrously big mallard duck waddled past. A man's hands protruded from either side like an extra pair of wings. The man's spectacled face was trapped within the duck's shoulders by a silver net. It was as if a duck had been grown around a man. The man's eyes were desperate. He said nothing.

There came a rush of tiny demons that looked like children mutated with frog DNA. A blue-faced gnome. A shriveled man pierced through and through with a tree branch. Small, swift, red-skinned demons with cat whiskers. A green dragon carrying a tall, smoldering torch.

They were nightmares of deformity. Perverse creations made of animals and body parts. Walking tableaux of pain and suffering. And worse, delight in pain and suffering.

There was no standing before them, no resistance possible, no way to hold on to any brave resolve.

Jobs felt his will dissolve in sheer, bloody panic. He turned and ran. He ran into Mo'Steel, who stood there, transfixed, horrified.

The impact stopped Jobs for just long enough.

"We have to get Billy!" Jobs yelled. He grabbed Mo'Steel's arm and shook him. "Get Billy! We have to get out of here."

"Got that right, Duck," Mo'Steel yelled, voice quavering.

They fumbled for the stretcher handles, hands shaking, eyes bulging. Demons were filling the room. There were screams, giddy laughter, groans of deep agony.

"Let's get out of here," Olga moaned, sounding like one of the poor, tortured creatures.

"They're just Cartoons," Violet said, but without conviction.

One of the little red demons darted forward and stabbed at Jobs with a sharp stick. Jobs dropped his grip on the stretcher and Billy slammed head-down. Jobs wailed and held up his arm, showing the bleeding cut.

The demon had skittered back, laughing and cavorting happily.

"Down the stairs!" Mo'Steel roared.

The Blue Meanie was already moving, heading for the stairs. But he stood aside as the panicked humans rushed past.

From behind, Jobs heard a whirring sound, metallic, sudden, short. Then screams of pain and rage and the heavy tread of the Blue Meanie chasing down the stairs after them.

The stairs didn't go far, maybe twenty feet to the

next lower level. This time Jobs saw the Meanie turn and raise one front leg or hand or whatever it was. The whirring sound came again and a cloud sprayed from the Meanie.

One of the demons, the fish-headed monstrosity, had descended the stairs. The Meanie's cloud hit and the demon was shredded.

Fléchettes, Jobs realized. The Meanie had fired a fléchette gun, thousands of tiny, sharp-edged shards that hit like buckshot.

The demons didn't follow, but that didn't stop the panicked flight. Through the only door. Down another stairway. Left. Left again and down farther.

Jobs felt as if he could keep running forever. The horrors were too fresh, too specific, not some vague nightmare feeling but things of flesh and blood that couldn't be, couldn't be anywhere outside of a psychotic's imagination.

But at last exhaustion stopped them. Jobs was sobbing with each breath. His throat was raw, his arms like lead, his feet felt battered. His heart would not slow down, would not stop the hammering.

They dropped Billy none too gently and collapsed onto the stone floor.

The Blue Meanie stayed with them, waited, watched.

Jobs raised himself on one elbow, looked fearfully around, saw no demons. He started to speak but knew his voice would come out shrill and hysterical. He closed his eyes, forced himself to think. They were Cartoons. Just Cartoons. Matter suspended and manipulated within very sophisticated force fields. The question of the science, the technology involved, calmed him.

"Okay, Violet," Jobs said, "what is this? Where are we?"

"Bosch," she said, eyes wide.

"What's that mean?"

"Hieronymus Bosch. He inspired Brueghel. But no one ever beat Bosch for coming up with weird, scary . . . for sheer fantasy, for strange and disturbing images . . . Did you see that back there? Do you know where those things are from?"

Jobs shook his head.

"They're from hell," Violet whispered. "A painting called *Last Judgment.* Bosch painted hell. And now we're in it."

CHAPTER ELEVEN

"HERE THEY COME! HERE THEY COME!"

2Face waited, ready for her move, but waiting for the right time.

Yago's goal was clear and simple: By dividing the group, he hoped to rule. It wasn't even subtle or original. It was high school. If he could decide who was in and who was out, he could basically create the "popular" clique. He would decide who was cool and who was uncool.

And just like any high school clique, the main criterion would be looks. Tamara and the baby were different, mutated, perhaps not entirely human. 2Face was deformed. Edward — unfortunately, Yago had finally noticed Jobs's little brother — was some kind of mutant.

So they were the early targets. If Yago could succeed in defining the four of them as outsiders, uncool, rejects, he would gain power.

That couldn't happen. Stopping it would be close to impossible. 2Face knew enough to know that there is no appeals process for being labeled an outsider, uncool, a dork, a freak, whatever. Once the label was applied it was almost impossible to scrape it off.

She couldn't count on her father for much. He didn't get it. Besides, he was lost in mourning for his wife, 2Face's mother. He was so preoccupied with one loss that he would do little to stop another one.

"Fine," 2Face told herself. "I'll take care of it myself."

And she knew how.

2Face was going to draw a line between herself and Tamara. Tamara and the baby were *real* freaks. 2Face was a victim of an accident. There was a difference.

If she could turn everyone against Tamara, she could save herself by becoming one of the persecutors instead of one of the persecuted.

It wasn't pretty or elegant. It wasn't moral. It would probably work.

Wylson had organized an early-warning system. T.R. and Tate had been sent down the ramp about three hundred yards. Half that distance away were

2Face's father and Anamull. If the Riders came, T.R. would yell to Shy and Shy would yell to the main group as both sets of sentries raced for cover.

It wouldn't provide much warning, but it would provide some.

That was it, 2Face had realized with a contemptuous sneer, that was all Wylson had managed to arrange. No doubt Wylson was a good businessperson. She was no general.

"I hear something," Burroway hissed from his position by the arch.

Then, everyone heard it: Anamull and Shy bellowing, "Here they come! Here they come!"

Every face was turned to Wylson.

Wylson was blank, staring. She licked her lips and glanced desperately at Tamara.

The time had come. 2Face said, "We only have one soldier."

Yago frowned, confused.

2Face plowed ahead quickly. "When they killed Errol the Riders took him on in single combat. Same when Tamara fought them downstairs. They seem to have some kind of code. Maybe some kind of alien chivalry."

"So what?" Yago asked, anxious to regain the initiative.

"So why doesn't Tamara challenge their leader, one on one?" 2Face said. "After all, not only is she a trained soldier, she's . . . she seems to have . . . some special powers. We all know she's *different.* Her and the baby both. Why don't they go challenge the Riders?"

The sentries came racing breathlessly in.

"What are we going to do?" Anamull wailed.

"How many are there?" Wylson asked.

"I don't know, like, like, ten," Tate said.

"More," Shy Hwang said, panting, hands on knees.

"Ritual single combat," 2Face said, trying to keep the desperation and self-loathing out of her voice. They were all that was left of *Homo sapiens.* All that was left of Earth. They could be building a new civilization. Instead they were playing high-school games. "It's the only way."

The baby cooed.

Tamara said, "We'll do it. We'll do it for free. This time. But if we win, well, there may be a next time. And next time, there'll be a price to be paid."

CHAPTER TWELVE

"DON'T MESS WITH A MAKER."

Sergeant Tamara Hoyle heard the words coming out of her mouth and they scared her.

"And next time, there'll be a price to be paid."

What did that mean? Why had she said it?

What was the baby up to?

She had grown accustomed to the presence of the baby inside her head. She could feel it all the time.

At the start, back when she had first awakened from hibernation, she'd believed it was the normal connection of mother to child. At first it had been a tendril touching her own consciousness. A gentle touch, welcome, pleasurable, reassuring.

Then they had cut her umbilical cord and the baby's touch had become a grasp. The tentative finger had become a fist.

At first she'd been confused. Not knowing what

was baby and what was Tamara. But as the baby's control had grown, she'd been more and more clear in her mind about what was Tamara and what was baby. There was very little now that was Tamara, except when the baby became bored or distracted.

The baby never ate.

The baby wasn't interested in small talk. The baby wasn't interested in the minute-by-minute matters that were handled by Tamara's brain. She was free to eat or not, sit, stand, sleep, smile, or frown. The baby had no interest in her as a person. The baby cared only for the serious decisions.

The baby had a goal, though Tamara didn't know what it was. She could sense it. She could feel the energy, the will. The baby was determined. The baby was confident, but scared, too.

Malice. That's what she felt from that other consciousness. Malice and intent and determination.

One thing Tamara knew, or thought she knew at least: The baby wasn't really interested in the Remnants. It had other goals and the humans were shadow figures, objects to be used or discarded.

All except Billy Weir. Billy was no shadow to the baby. Billy was bright and sharp-edged and dangerous. But Billy was no longer here.

The others . . . Yago, Wylson, 2Face, all of them with their transparent games, they were all beside the point. The baby played a different game.

What *was* the baby?

Tamara didn't know. She thought she saw parts of herself in him, parts of his father. She wanted the baby to be her own flesh and blood. It was. It wasn't. Her feelings changed from hour to hour. It was human, it wasn't. It was something else. Something unnatural, or perhaps a natural result of the terribly unnatural circumstances of its birth.

She'd been shot, wounded, collapsed. She'd been placed into hibernation, shot and pregnant.

And five hundred years later she'd been revived and the wound was healed and the baby had been born. How long ago? And how had it been born at all from a body that was, to all intents and purposes, dead?

An unnatural natural consequence of unnatural circumstances. A mutation. An adaptation.

Or something else.

Either way, the baby was in her mind, and she could not resist it.

And when she'd fought the Rider, when she'd done battle, she'd had strength and speed that she knew had not come from her Marine Corps training or her rigorous fitness routine. It was wonderful. Whatever the source, it was wonderful.

Power. From somewhere else.

She felt it now as she sauntered out through the arch. Felt the calm that power brings.

Tamara had placed the baby inside the arch. It didn't matter. The baby's control did not rely on touch.

Tamara shouldered the spear, nonchalant, and stepped out onto the ramp. She took up a stance, legs apart, knees slightly bent, free hand resting on hip.

The Riders — she counted six, not the ten or dozen that Anamull and Shy had imagined. They were skimming along on their hoverboards, holding in a rough line abreast.

It was happening again. A weirdness in her vision. Like she could see a million miles. No, that wasn't it, either. It wasn't super vision, just different vision. She saw the Riders in detail, detail that went below the skin and the bone. She saw them down to their muscles and tendons. It was as if she could see the very nerves, the connection that ran from brain to hand, from hand back to brain.

She saw into and through the Riders. She felt she

could almost see the thoughts taking shape in their heads.

The Riders saw her and reined in their hover-boards.

"Hi, boys," Tamara said. "Nice night, huh?"

The Riders glared at her. They could glare, the Riders could. They stared at her with an array of insect eyes, small and large. The writhing snake head, the second head, though Tamara knew it was not a true head, more like an animated mouth, gnashed razor teeth.

The lead Rider — you could tell because the leader's hoverboard bore a series of small blue daubs attached to the leading edge — let loose the earsplitting shriek.

Tamara did not quail. She pointed one long finger at her own chest, then turned it to the leader. "You and me." She spread her hands wide to make the invitation clear. Right here, right now, one-on-one.

The Rider's face turned a darker shade of rust. Anger? No, the baby knew, worry. The Rider's eating head extended a black tongue and tasted the air. Anxiety.

Behind her, Tamara could sense and hear the group gathered in the archway, the bolder ones, anyway. The baby was there. Tamara could see the scene through his eyes. His impossible, eyeless eyes. She could see herself, all alone, before the towering, hovering Riders.

The baby laughed.

Tamara cocked her head. "Well? You here to fight or just to enjoy the view?"

The Rider could not possibly understand her words, of course, but he knew that he was being mocked.

A guttural series of clicks issued from his mouth and the other Riders withdrew, forming a semicircle a hundred feet behind their leader.

Now the blood surged through Tamara's muscles. Now the nerves tingled. Now her every sense was trained, not on the Rider's face or arms, but within him, down into his core.

He would strike with his boomerang.

A flick of movement and a curved, toothed stick flew. It was thrown at Tamara's head, but meant to miss. It was a trick: The return flight of the boomerang would slice her neck.

Tamara didn't flinch as the boomerang passed the first time. She waited, eyes on the Rider. The boomerang curved and returned without any seeming loss of blinding speed. Tamara could hear its *flit-flit-flit* sound.

She stuck her spear back, slapped the boomerang's leading edge, killing its speed. It dropped straight down and she caught it in her free hand and threw it back without drawing breath.

The boomerang flew. The Rider chief dodged. The boomerang flew on and caught one of the other Riders full in his face.

A shriek of pain. The injured Rider fell from his hoverboard, landed hard. He tore at the boomerang, firmly wedged into his main head, just between the large upper eyes and the smaller lower eyes.

The chief glanced back at his fallen comrade.

"Yeah," Tamara said with a laugh that echoed from the baby.

The chief surged at her, slid back on his board, and used the underside of the board as a battering ram.

The board shot through unoccupied space. Tamara leaped straight up, high, impossibly high, more than her own height. She sliced her spear horizontally. Missed! The Rider chief had dodged just in time.

Tamara fell, but as she fell she ripped the spear point down and scored a deep cut on the Rider's left forefoot.

She landed, stabbed up and at an angle, and buried the point of her spear in the chief's lower belly, just beneath the beetle carapace.

Things began to happen to her. Things that those who watched would never later be able to explain or even sequence.

She rolled beneath the chief's hoverboard and threw her spear. It hit one of the Riders and skewered his eating head.

On her back, upward kick, she connected with the back edge of the wounded chief's unstable hoverboard. The chief toppled off and landed face first in the dust. His board shot away, unguided.

Tamara back somersaulted, landed, kicked, and flew high to land with both boots planted on the chief's shoulders. There was a crunching sound, a bundle of twigs being snapped. She snatched the chief's scimitar and ran, screaming, straight at the remaining four Riders.

She leaped with far more than human muscle and flew at the nearest Rider, sword point straight out in front. The Rider backed up, reared back, and Tamara changed direction in midair.

Changed direction without touching anything. Part of her mind registered this fact as impossible. And yet, her wild leap changed direction like some mad curveball and she swept her scimitar across and sliced both heads from one of the Riders.

The last three uninjured Riders turned their hoverboards and raced away at full speed, shrieking, yowling.

Tamara landed easily and calmly walked back to the chief, who was fatally injured, but was taking a while to accept that fact.

Tamara knelt by him and looked down at him with interest, right into his faceted, emotionless eyes.

"Don't mess with a Maker," she whispered.

"Get their weapons," she instructed the slack-jawed onlookers.

She winked at 2Face, gathered up the baby, and only with greatest effort of will concealed the exhaustion that was like the ground opening up to swallow her.

CHAPTER THIRTEEN

"MOTHER IS CONFUSED."

"They're coming down the steps!" Violet said tersely.

Jobs had seen them. The demons, the tittering, creepy, skin-crawling mob of them were shadowing the humans, following. Lower, always lower. Every path going up was blocked. Every door leading to the outside was filled with demons.

Impossible not to conclude that the demons were herding them. Guiding them ever lower. Down and down. To some inferno? To some vision of hell?

Jobs resented it. Beyond being scared, he resented it. *This is what came of superstition,* he told himself, knowing he was being unreasonable. Some late-Middle-Ages painter didn't know his painting would become a real-life horror a billion miles away from Earth. Still, Jobs resented it. This is what came of believing nonsense.

The Blue Meanie had become a part of the group. It wasn't something anyone had decided, it had just happened. They moved together, Jobs, Mo'Steel, Violet, Olga, Billy, and now the Meanie.

Down stone steps. Across echoing chambers. Through doors. Around open wells that might go down forever.

No, Jobs reminded himself, the wells didn't go down forever. They could go no farther than the outer hull of the ship. This was a ship. This was not some version of hell wrapped up inside the Tower of Babel. This was the ship's attempt to invent an environment based on input it could not possibly understand.

The ship — whether person or machine — was merely using the data it had available. It probably didn't even understand that the data was art, not some representation of reality. The ship was building a world for them, for humans, and may not know that it was using data derived from an outrageous imagination.

That's what Jobs tried to tell himself, but a different feeling was growing, a suspicion. What rational creature could fail to see the difference between fact and fiction? The ship, the alien or computer, or whatever it was, could see actual humans, could see what they were, how they looked, how they moved, spoke, ate, drank. Surely the ship noticed that there was a disconnect between the actual humans and the artistic re-creations of them. Surely in all the terabytes of data the ship had downloaded from the shuttle, all the culture and history, the books and photos and recordings, surely the ship had been able to figure out what was real and what was not.

The ship was messing with them. That's what Jobs felt, though he couldn't prove it. The ship had an agenda. The ship was up to something.

Or else the ship was just stupid.

Could it — machine or organism — be this powerful and sophisticated and yet be stupid? Possible. Termites made huge mounds, self-contained civilizations of enormous complexity, but no termite had yet learned to read.

Powerful and stupid? Was the ship some sort of intelligence so profoundly alien that it simply couldn't understand the data? Could only plug it in and hope for the best?

"We need a rest," Jobs said.

Mo'Steel nodded. "I have blisters on my blisters."

"Okay, right here, then," Jobs said and he set down the stretcher none too gently. He was also bitterly resenting Billy now. The guy should either wake up or die. Instead he lay there like a vegetable.

"Let's close that door at least," Olga said. She slammed a wooden door behind them. It would only delay the appearance of the demons who would eventually arrive via a stairway to the left or perhaps appear in the following open door.

Jobs lay back flat on the cool stone. The Meanie stopped, stood apart, but did not move away.

"How is there light in here?" Jobs wondered. "There's no light source."

Violet said, "There's no painting without light."

"We're in a maze," Mo'Steel said. He jerked a thumb at the Blue Meanie. "Maybe he knows where we are."

"Why don't you ask him?" Jobs said, snappish.

Violet sat hugging her legs to her. In his present resentful mood Jobs was glad at least that the "Jane" had not managed to find anything to sit on but floor.

"We should never have left the shuttle," Jobs muttered, daring anyone to argue the point. No one took the bait.

"I kind of hate to bring this up," Mo'Steel said awkwardly. "But I need some privacy."

Jobs shot him a frown, then realized what Mo'Steel was talking about. "Just turn away."

"Not that. The other," Mo'Steel said primly.

"Sweetie, it's a natural thing, we all have to go," Olga said.

Mo'Steel blushed and glanced at Violet.

Jobs rolled his eyes. The truth was, he could use some privacy himself. But the room was nothing but bare, blank stone. There was a well, one of the open holes on the far side of the chamber, but there was nothing blocking it off.

"We'll all turn away," Olga said. "Miss Blake? We're all turning away."

Violet shook herself out of a reverie. "Excuse me?"

"We're all turning away. That way," Olga repeated.

"Ah," Violet said, grasping the situation at last.

Mo'Steel moved off and Jobs focused his attention on the alien. The Blue Meanie stood at rest. He seemed to be looking, insofar as he could be said to be looking at anything particular, at Billy. And once again, Billy's lips were moving silently.

Suddenly the Meanie reared up, not standing on its hind legs, but seeming to lengthen its front legs to bare the oval panel on its chest.

This again, Jobs thought.

The panel brightened. Like a low-wattage light had gone on behind it.

A stream of letters and symbols appeared, racing by.

"Hey!" Jobs yelled. "Look at this."

The letters scrolled, widened to fill the screen, shrank, split into multiple lines, then resolved back to one. The scroll slowed. Individual letters could be seen, then clusters forming nonsense words.

Then . . .

I AM FOUR SACRED STREAMS.

Jobs was on his feet. Violet came and stood beside him.

"It's communicating," Violet said.

"It's writing," Jobs agreed. "How? And what are we supposed to do, write back? We don't have anything with a keyboard."

"Or pen and paper," Violet added.

"Yeah, that would have worked, too, I guess," Jobs said. He yelled, "Mo! Are you done? The Meanie's communicating."

"Can I have a minute here?" Mo'Steel yelled back, sounding uncharacteristically petulant.

"My name is Violet Blake," Violet said to the alien.

No answer. The message remained fixed: *I AM FOUR SACRED STREAMS.*

"Maybe that's all the language it's acquired," Jobs suggested.

Mo'Steel rejoined the group, refusing to meet anyone's eye. Another time Jobs would have been amused by his friend's embarrassment. Mo'Steel wasn't just old-fashioned, he was positively Victorian.

"What's up?" Mo'Steel asked.

Jobs pointed at the glowing oval and the five printed words.

"Huh," Mo'Steel said. "Is that his name? Like a Native American name? Or is he saying he actually is four streams?"

"Four streams of what?" Olga wondered.

"Sacred streams," Violet said with a shrug. "Oh!"

The message had changed.

MEANING UNDERSTOOD VIOLET BLAKE.

"How does he know my name?" she wondered.

"You told him," Jobs pointed out. "A few minutes ago. You said, 'I'm Violet Blake.' It just took him this long to decipher your response."

"It's hard to see how we'll ever have a good conversation at this speed," Violet said.

Jobs knelt down beside Billy. He turned so he could see the alien and the boy at the same time. "Hello, Four Sacred Streams. What is your species called?"

Billy Weir slowly, silently repeated the words. It took a long time. The alien replied.

WE ARE THE CHILDREN. THE TRUE CHILDREN OF MOTHER.

"Doesn't clear up much," Mo'Steel said. "We're all our Mother's children."

But Jobs smiled, deeply happy. He gently smoothed Billy's hair. "Good job, Billy. Ask him what he wants."

This time Billy's lips did not move. The answer came immediately.

I MUST STOP TRANSMISSIONS FROM THIS NODE.

Jobs was more surprised by the speed of response and Billy's failure to mouth the question. Touch? Was that it?

Jobs pulled his hand away from Billy. "Ask him what he means by node."

Billy began mouthing the words, slowly, painfully slowly.

NODE 31 PROJECTS THIS ENVIRONMENT.

Jobs held his breath, touched his hand to Billy's arm, and said, "Why must you stop transmission from this node?"

The reply was immediate.

THIS ENVIRONMENT WILL KILL ME, the Meanie wrote. Then it added, *THIS ENVIRONMENT WILL KILL YOU.*

Jobs felt his hand trembling. He was communicating with an alien species. How he was doing so he couldn't say. He'd worry about that later. "Are you saying this ship is trying to kill us?"

MOTHER WILL KILL US.

"Is . . . when you say 'Mother' do you mean the ship? Is the ship Mother?"

Yes.

"Why would the . . . why would Mother want to kill us?"

MOTHER IS, the Meanie wrote, then hesitated over the next word before adding, *CONFUSED.*

Jobs frowned, intent on getting to some understanding. But just then the demons reappeared, a rush of them, running down the steps, led now by a tall, painfully thin man with a bare skull for a head. Mo'Steel yelped.

"Mother has to have downloaded Monet, Utrillo, Cézanne, O'Keeffe . . . but she picks Bosch?" Violet complained.

COMMUNICATE MORE LATER, Four Sacred Streams said.

"Yeah. Run now, talk later," Mo'Steel agreed.

CHAPTER FOURTEEN

"THE CHAMELEON."

Bad move, 2Face told herself. It had been a monumentally bad move.

She had tried to save herself by sacrificing Tamara and the baby. She had played the game of high-school politics and lost. Tamara owned the group now; no one was going to expel her. Tamara was the toughest kid in school now. She had respect.

Which left 2Face and Edward as the designated freaks.

With the threat of the Riders receding, Yago would make his move against 2Face. He would win. 2Face would lose and become the all-purpose goat. It was inevitable.

In this place, scared, disoriented, hungry and thirsty, and with shaky leadership, the people were reverting to more primitive models. Good-bye to liberal civilization with its tolerance and inclusiveness. Scared, powerless people needed scapegoats. Yago knew this and Yago knew that the one who is different is always the first choice to play the role of scapegoat.

Burn the witch.

2Face touched her face. Touched the crenellated line where whole flesh met scar tissue. Another few weeks and she'd have been through the surgery and treatment. Another few weeks and she would have been normal.

She'd made a virtue of being a freak, back on Earth. In a place where ugliness was merely a curable medical condition, her jarring, disconcerting face was almost a statement: Look, here's pain, here's ugliness, deal with it.

In tame, secure, enlightened, early-twenty-first-century America, it was safe enough to be provocative and different. This place was a long way from all that.

2Face looked at the others, scanning, hoping to find some angle she could work. She had to avoid becoming "the other," the outsider. The only way to do that was to find a substitute victim. She'd tried to make Tamara that victim, but that was before Tamara had single-handedly slaughtered the Riders.

2Face knew what she was thinking was wrong. Obviously it was wrong. Or would be, back in the world, but here she was fighting for her life. She was the freak. She was the ugly one. By the relentless logic of Yago's need, 2Face would be the one to be shunned, excluded, blamed, and vilified.

2Face slumped, head in hands. Yago was carefully not looking in her direction. He was waiting till the rush of the victory had worn off. He was waiting for his moment. Hours? A day, even?

He hated her for nothing, for a casual blow-off way back on Earth. And for being smart enough to see him as he was.

2Face rocked slowly back and forth on her heels, glared at her father, raged at him silently. Didn't he know they'd go for him next? He was the father of the freak, after all.

Only one thing to do. Only one way. She had to leave. Walk now, before they could make her run. Go to Jobs and his group — if they were still alive somewhere.

Exile. Take Edward and go to Jobs. It would be humiliating, but 2Face could work with Jobs and Mo'Steel. Even that "Jane," Miss Blake.

No other way.

But how? Which way? Not through that little

door, that was for sure. The only way was out onto the ramp.

She got up and found Edward. "Edward, we have to go."

"Where?"

"We're going to find your brother."

"Sebastian?"

2Face frowned. "Sebastian? Oh, is that Jobs's birth name?"

"Yeah. His name is Sebastian. Only sometimes people call him Jobs."

"A good name to change," 2Face muttered. "Okay, look, I need you to do something first, before we can go. You know that thing where you kind of make yourself look like whatever is around you?"

Edward stared blankly. "What?"

"That chameleon thing. You kind of blend in. I need you to do that because we have to take the spear that Ms. Lefkowitz-Blake has, okay? See the spear? The long, pointy thing leaning against the wall by her?"

Edward rolled his eyes. "I know what a spear is, 2Face. But what were you saying about chameleons?"

"Edward, sometimes you seem to kind of change a little and look like the stuff around you. Didn't you know? Your skin and even your clothes and all will kind of look like the walls or whatever is near."

Edward looked down at himself, searching for some evidence of this. He found a gray line that ran up his arm. He touched the line and looked up at 2Face in wonder. "It's like the line between the stones."

2Face nodded. "Yes, it is."

"How did this happen?"

He looked as if he might start crying. 2Face took his hand and held it. "Hey, look, it's not a bad thing. I mean . . . hey, don't you ever watch cartoons or whatever about superheroes? Spider-Man? This is like a superpower you have."

Edward looked unsure, teetering on the edge between crying or embracing this new idea. His eyes went shrewd. "A superpower?"

"Yeah." 2Face nodded and winked. "Now, look, we need you to get that spear. Try not to let anyone see you. Or at least not notice you."

"The Chameleon," Edward said, trying out the name.

"Whatever. Get the spear. We need some kind of weapon. Meet me just outside the archway. I'm going to grab one of those meat pies. We need to move fast."

Edward headed toward the spear, stopped, looked back, saw 2Face's encouraging smile, and opted to creep along the wall.

Not a true chameleon, 2Face thought. Not yet, anyway. He still looked like the boy he was; he didn't look like the wall. It was just that his skin color changed somehow. He blended in. It was like a soldier in camouflage — the camouflage didn't make you look like a bush, but it made it hard for the human eye to pick you out.

Edward was helped by the fact that Wylson had decided to call yet another meeting of her board of directors, or whatever she called it. The adults plus Yago.

2Face saw her father, head bowed under the weight of his grief, join the group. His every physical movement broadcast the fact that he would make no trouble for anyone, that he was lost in his own world.

2Face was furious with him. But at the same time, the prospect of setting out alone in this terrifying place, maybe never seeing him again, was daunting. She'd lost too much to want to lose any more.

Edward was standing by the arch, spear in hand. 2Face herself had lost sight of him at some point.

She shook herself, tried to push away the intruding edge of self-pity, and went to Edward.

No one cried out to stop them as they stepped, alone, onto the ramp.

"Up or down, left or right?" 2Face wondered.

To the right, downhill, were the remains of the slaughtered Riders.

"Up it is."

CHAPTER FIFTEEN

"BACK TO THE SHIP."

2Face and Edward walked up the ramp. The world was dark, stars were few, and the moon was nowhere in sight. But the ramp, the very ground under their feet, seemed to glow enough to remain visible.

At any moment a troop of Riders might loom up in front of them and then, 2Face knew, it would all be over very quickly. She was not Tamara. She could not fight and win, despite the comforting heft of the spear in her hand.

She looked back from time to time, half expecting pursuit. Yago would be furious: He'd be deprived of his intended victims.

It was a victory for 2Face, but a pitifully small one.

They walked for a time, maybe a half hour, maybe less. And now 2Face was just weary. The rush of escape was long past and the exhaustion was causing her feet to stumble and the spear to lie very heavy on her shoulder.

"You're probably tired," she said to Edward. "Anyway, we won't find Jobs in the dark, right, kid?"

"I guess not."

"Okay, well, let's see if we can find a place to lie down."

There was an archway, one of the endless series of archways always to their left, always threatening. "We can't lie down out here in the open," 2Face said, trying to convince herself. Truth was, neither choice looked good. Out in the open they might be seen by Riders. But who knew what lay beyond any of the arches?

2Face hushed Edward unnecessarily and strained to hear. Nothing. She stepped closer to the dark, open door. Nothing inside.

"I'm scared," Edward said.

"Don't be scared," 2Face said. "The Riders will worry about the main group back there. They don't even know we're here, right?"

She took Edward's hand and led him through the archway.

Her foot landed on nothing and she pitched forward. Instinctively she tightened her grip on Edward and drew him after her. They fell, tumbling, head over heels, screaming, falling farther than she had ever fallen before. Long seconds, flashes of dark red shapes, eerie forms, and still they fell.

Smothering!

2Face had fallen into something sticky, into and through something that felt like warm taffy covering her entire body. She couldn't breathe.

Then, air! She sucked in deeply. Air. She could breathe and see and yet she felt the sticky, pliable covering over her entire body, every square inch and —

She fell away from the ship. Fell into space. Fell toward a raging inferno of exploding gas. A billion nuclear explosions. A sky-filling, universe-filling mass of seething yellow and orange fire.

She slowed, stopped, hung in midair, only it was not sky but space.

The ship was above her. The hole she'd fallen out of closed and disappeared. With a psychic wrench that left her wanting to be sick, the ship above became the ship below. Her perspective shifted and now she was floating above the ship, above a vast, endless topography of dull metallic extrusions, and glowing bubbles, and snapping arcs of what seemed to be red and purple neon.

It was impossible to understand. Impossible to make sense of.

Above her head now, the star. So close she could see whirlpools in the superheated gases, trembling seas of light, and sudden volcanic eruptions that shot planet-sized streamers into space.

The star seemed close enough that she could reach out and touch it. She held up her hand and saw clearly the transparent goo that covered her, that fed her oxygen, that bled away the blowtorch-tip heat, that she hoped and prayed would shield her from the murderous storm of radiation.

She saw Edward, just a few feet away, like herself encased, like herself staring wide-eyed.

The ship was passing so close to the star that it could only be deliberate. The galaxy was a big place and so empty that all the stars and planets together didn't amount to more than dust. Yet, here she was, within cosmic millimeters of a star.

The ship slid past the star, fast enough that 2Face could actually see the star passing by beneath them like the ground seen through a car window. It was an impossible speed. A speed unlike anything any human had achieved.

2Face cried out in awe. She was an insect

crushed between hammer and anvil. A cinder twirling above the fire.

Suddenly two massive pillars of blinding yellow light stabbed from star to ship. It was impossible to tell the size because it was impossible to tell the distance, but 2Face felt their vastness, felt them to be miles thick, an energy stream of sufficient power to light Earth forever.

Just as suddenly the beams of light terminated. The ship had replenished its energy.

2Face found she was panting, gasping. Not for lack of air but overwhelmed, stunned.

"Back. I have to get back," she said and heard her voice vibrate through the bone.

She began floating back down, falling in slow motion toward the ship. How? A body in motion . . .

What had moved her?

"Have to get Edward," she said, once again feeling rather than hearing her own voice.

She began to drift toward Edward, who still stared at the sun.

He could go blind, 2Face thought, but at the same time she realized that she had not. The goo, the film around her had shielded her eyes.

Some kind of space suit for going outside the ship. That was clear enough. She and Edward had fallen down a hole that must have been part of the original architecture of the ship, not part of its art-derived artificial environment.

Whoever had built the ship must use the wells as a quick means for exiting the ship. The gooey suit was applied automatically.

Why? For the ship's crew to do maintenance? Surely not. A ship this advanced must have easier ways to deal with external maintenance.

And was it mere coincidence that the ship was passing so close to a star? What were the odds?

Sight-seeing? Was that it? Was the ship merely providing her with an awesome sight? Jump down the well and see a star up close and personal from the cozy safety of a high-tech space suit?

A trickle of suspicion. A ship with the power to create vast artificial environments, a ship that allowed passengers to literally jump out into space as she had done? It was like an amusement park: rides and Sims and animatrons. It was Disney World and Universal Studios.

Surely not. That couldn't be it. Who built a ship this vast for entertainment?

2Face reached Edward. She tapped him with a goo-covered hand. "Edward. Can you hear me?"

He turned in response to her touch. When he

spoke she could not hear his words. She motioned back to the ship. She mouthed the words, "Back to the ship."

The two floating bodies began falling once more, slow but steady. The visual field shifted once more as 2Face's brain struggled to cope with the irrational. Her stomach lurched and she vomited.

The vomit passed through the goo. In seconds it steamed and evaporated, leaving nothing but a smudge of dust behind.

Now the ship was definitely above her once more and she felt herself no longer to be falling, but rather being sucked upward. The hole, or at least a hole, appeared again.

Together 2Face and Edward fell/rose toward a round, black cave.

Shadow wrapped around them, the hatch closed, the absolute loss of the star's light left 2Face feeling blind.

She could feel the goo covering sliding away, slipping off her body, puddling, and then whisking off on its own.

A current of warm air billowed beneath her and she and Edward floated upward.

"That was cool," Edward said.

CHAPTER SIXTEEN

"GET UP OFF YOUR KNEES AND DEAL WITH IT."

It was one thing for Jobs to act like the demons were just figments of someone's imagination. Mo'Steel wasn't so sure. Who was to say that Bosch or whatever his name was, the old, dead artist, who was to say that he hadn't gotten a sneak peek at what the real, actual hell looked like?

If these things creeping and slithering and chattering in the dark weren't actual demons, actual residents of the inferno, they were close enough. They were all that Mo'Steel's grandmother had ever led him to expect of the real, actual hell.

He hadn't heard much about such things from his parents. The whole family was Catholic, but Mo'Steel's mother and father were Catholic by way of M.I.T. and U.C. Santa Cruz and Northwestern University. His nana was Catholic by way of a tiny village in the Chiapas region of Mexico.

Olga would have been shocked and a little offended to find such ideas occupying a place in her son's mind. But Nana's stories had made a bigger impact than Olga's lukewarm reassurances.

Mo'Steel had always favored the more extreme version of just about any story. Eternal damnation wasn't much of a peril in Olga's version of events. Like jumping over a puddle as opposed to leaping a bottomless canyon. Nana's view was extreme and bizarre and imaginative, and Mo'Steel liked his risks big. A desire for comfort and security had never registered with Mo'Steel.

Nana had an imagination. She had been a cleaning woman most of her life, married to a handyman. She looked older than she was, probably. To Mo'Steel she looked about ninety, though that couldn't be the truth.

And Nana told great stories. She could have been a writer. But she'd come up with nothing any weirder and more disturbing than the distorted, insane, absurd, half-man, half-beast things that shadowed Mo'Steel and his friends through the Tower of Babel.

That's what made Mo'Steel wonder if they might not be real. At least real in the sense that the artist had somehow gotten a glimpse of the actual hell.

He didn't mention any of this out loud. Jobs would have rolled his eyes. Olga would have made a face. Violet would have patiently explained that what they were confronting was only an animated version of a painter's vision.

Mo'Steel wondered about Billy Weir, though. What did he think of it? What did he see?

"Always down," Jobs muttered, not for the first time. "They're definitely forcing us downward."

"Our alien friend seems not to object to the direction," Olga observed.

"Why don't they just move in and force us to fight?" Jobs wondered.

"Because the devil don't live in the attic, 'migo," Mo'Steel said.

"What?"

"Nothing."

"I wonder how far down we've come?" Jobs asked no one in particular. "There has to be a bottom eventually."

"Four-hundred-nineteen steps," Mo'Steel said. "The risers probably average about nine inches, so that's three-thousand-seven-hundred-seventy-one inches, or three-hundred-fourteen feet and three inches."

"That's quite a talent," Violet said. "Do you do square roots?"

Mo'Steel grinned. "Pick a number."

"Four hundred and seventy-one."

Mo'Steel considered for a moment. "Twenty-one point seven oh two five."

"How do you do that?"

Mo'Steel shrugged. "In goes the question, out pops the answer. Just one of those things."

Olga came over and gave her son a walking hug. "I should have had you earlier. You could have helped me through calc."

Mo'Steel felt his mother trembling. She kept glancing back at the pursuing shadow.

So, Mo'Steel thought, *Nana told you some stories, too.*

"More stairs," Violet reported from slightly ahead.

The demon army edged in closer now, just a few arm's-lengths away. A wall of grinning, insinuating, leering, deformed faces.

The Blue Meanie limped down the stairs at an unhurried pace. "It's lighter down there," Violet reported.

Mo'Steel shifted his grip on the stretcher. He glanced back at Jobs, who shook his head, indicating that he didn't need a rest.

Mo'Steel saw the Blue Meanie below. He'd

stopped. He was waiting for them to catch up. The mirrored surface of his armor gleamed.

They started down the stairs. The demons set up a sudden loud, triumphant squall of catcalls and laughter and curses, and Mo'Steel almost dropped his hold on the stretcher.

They reached the bottom of the stairs and were no longer in a blank stone chamber.

In the distance, what looked very much like an old picture of a bombed-out Berlin from World War II. Wrecked buildings, smoldering fires, a landscape buried in ash, air full of sparks, shadows within shadows. Within the blasted landscape Mo'Steel could see things moving, writhing, like maggots on a piece of meat.

Closer at hand, a more vivid nightmare. Scenes of torture, scenes of horror, sights that made the flesh creep and the mind recoil.

At the base of a tree a hand reached up out of the dirt, a hand belonging to someone buried alive, a hand that beckoned for recusal.

On the flat tabletop roof of a low building scurried a creature with a white-bearded human head that seemed to be attached with a sharp stick to two scurrying rat legs.

Two men were yoked to a massive red millstone.

They pulled it around and around on a spiked turntable. Where the millstone should have been crushing wheat it crushed people.

An army of goblins drove herds of starved men while others were swallowed into the dirt or cooked alive or . . .

Mo'Steel dropped the stretcher from numb hands.

There was a sound coming from him, a low keening sound, a weird unnatural sound like nothing his own voice could produce.

Mo'Steel backed up the stairs, slipped, and fell hard. He turned and on hands and knees scrabbled up, stopped when he saw the army of demons descending toward him.

Mo'Steel heard Jobs's voice coming from somewhere, far away, another planet, a million miles from this place.

"Strap it up, Mo, strap it up."

Mo'Steel couldn't answer, could only wail, could only cringe and cry.

He felt someone holding his head and heard singing. Singing that couldn't begin to drown out the screams and shrieks and cries of agony from everywhere.

His mother was holding him, rocking him, but she was crying, too, whimpering like him.

Suddenly rough hands shoved Olga away. A startling slap. A sharp pain on his face. Another slap. Another.

And then all he saw was Violet Blake's furious face, right in his.

"We already have one coma patient, we don't need another," Violet barked. "It's just a painting. It's just a painting. Get up off your knees and deal with it."

Mo'Steel stared, uncomprehending.

Violet Blake slapped him again and winced at the pain it caused her. "Move!" she yelled, furious, red in the face. "Get up and move!"

Mo'Steel stood up on shaky legs. He moved.

CHAPTER SEVENTEEN

"WE HAVE TO RUN. CAN YOU RUN?"

Edward looked at his arm. It was dark, gray, kind of rough-looking. Like gravel kind of. Like the walls and floor around him.

Too weird.

The Chameleon.

2Face was saying something; he only listened in bits and pieces. Something about how they were lost. Hello? Of course they were lost.

They should have stayed on Earth. Everyone said there was no way to survive, but how about digging really deep tunnels, or those places where they stored nuclear waste? Those were deep tunnels.

It had to be better than this place. At least there weren't Riders.

Edward turned his thoughts away from the Riders. They scared him and he didn't like being scared. His mom should be here. Sebastian said she was dead. His dad, too. But Edward hadn't seen them himself.

Another thing not to think about.

Why was this place so creepy? There were all these little sounds, these little scurrying sounds. Rats maybe.

That was okay. He was the Chameleon. A superhero.

"It's like some kind of a maze!" 2Face raged, speaking loudly, too loudly. "Every time we start off going one direction, we end up going another direction."

The Chameleon. That would be cool. Wasn't there a superhero by that name already? Probably. But Edward was real, not made up. And anyway, there were no TV shows or comic books here.

TV. That would be great. TV.

And some of his friends. Like . . .

Edward frowned. He couldn't immediately recall any of his friends. Hadn't he had friends? He must have. He remembered the feeling of having friends.

Oswald. He was a friend.

Yeah, like in kindergarten.

There had to have been friends. Definitely. Anyway, there was TV and some of the people on TV were like friends.

"I don't know what to do," 2Face said. "We're

lost. I know I shouldn't tell you that, being a little kid or whatever, but we're lost. I didn't really think this through, you know? This tower is so big. It's like . . . like being an ant lost inside the world's biggest beehive or whatever, just rooms and rooms and rooms and they're all pretty much the same."

Edward glanced at 2Face. Her normal face was toward him now as they walked along. Edward was disappointed. He kind of liked her melted face. It was cool. It was creepy and gross, but he was used to it. It was something creepy that he could deal with because it was her face, because he knew what it was, what it meant.

"We need to find your brother!" 2Face practically shouted.

She was scared, Edward knew. That's why she was talking so loud. He could tell from the way she kept touching her face. From the way she kept twisting her hands together.

"Do you think that was the sun?" Edward asked.

"What?" 2Face was confused.

"Was it the sun? Our sun, I mean?"

"Oh. The star?" She shrugged. "I don't know. Maybe. I don't know. How would I know? I've never flown like ten feet away from a star, so it's not like I could say, 'Oh, look, it's Aunt Dora's house down there, this must be good old Sol.' "

"Who's that?"

"Aunt Dora?"

"No." Edward pointed. "Him."

It was standing there staring at them. A deer, only walking standing up like a person. It had big antlers and a red cape.

Deer Man. What superpowers did Deer Man have?

"Back up," 2Face whispered. She reached out for him, took his arm, and squeezed too tight. But as they backed up they heard a sound and spun to face a thing, a creature, with the face of a bird, with a strangely long, sharp beak. The bird creature, too, was walking upright.

The two apparitions just stared. The deer blinked. Stared. No one breathed, no one spoke. 2Face dug her fingers into Edward's arm.

"Just edge away," she said. "Come on. Follow me. Slowly. Slowly."

They backed away, keeping an equal distance between themselves and the demons.

The Bird Man cocked his head sideways, exactly like an inquisitive robin.

Back, through an open archway. Then 2Face released Edward. He rubbed his arm.

"We have to run," she said. "Can you run?"

"Sure."

"Stay with me. And run!"

They took off as fast as they could run, Edward straining to keep up with shorter legs. And now that he was running the panic took hold. He glanced back, no one was chasing them, but it didn't matter, he could feel eyes watching him, could feel his skin tingling as if he were pursued by a cold wind, felt the hair on his neck stand up, felt his heart trip and miss beats.

The sound of their running feet echoed. 2Face panting. Edward panting. Running. A set of stairs. Up!

They stopped suddenly. A new monster, a thing made of a screaming, yellow head, barely human, with fire shooting sparks from a hole in its skull. It had no body, just lizard legs starting where its neck should be.

"Back!"

They tumbled back down the stairs, fleeing the hideous thing, trying to outrun fear.

"Run! Run!" 2Face shouted, and this time when Edward looked back, he saw them. Monsters of every description. Things with animal heads and reptile bodies, creatures with absurd boots and body parts that became clay pitchers pouring water or blood. A monster with a distorted, freakish green cat's head swallowing a human body, swallowing the legs as it bounded along.

Edward couldn't breathe. He was slowing down and 2Face was pulling ahead. The monsters would get him, the monsters would get him.

"Wait," he cried. "Wait for me!" And 2Face disappeared from sight, through a doorway filled with night.

CHAPTER EIGHTEEN

"KILLER EARS? KILLER EARS? WAS THIS GUY ON DRUGS?"

Jobs was stunned by Mo'Steel's collapse. Not that he wasn't due. But Mo'Steel was the Man of Steel. He leaped tall buildings with a single bound. Or tried to. He had jumped out of airplanes, snowboarded off cliffs, surfed with sharks.

That he would be scared, sure. Any sane person would be. But didn't Mo'Steel understand how much everyone was relying on him? He was the strong one. Jobs was supposed to be the analytical one; Mo'Steel was the tough one, the fearless one.

Or maybe not. Maybe Miss Blake was.

Jobs shot her a look. She was grim. Her lips were colorless, her entire face drawn tight. *She seemed angry,* Jobs thought, *angry at herself.*

And scared, but that went without saying.

The Blue Meanie was in the lead. Jobs wanted to

talk to it, ask it to explain. Maybe get some reassurance.

The demons were close around them now. They crowded close. But they hadn't attacked yet, not since earlier when Jobs had suffered the slight stab wound. Maybe the Cartoons remembered the Blue Meanie's fléchette gun.

Too many questions. Why would Cartoons fear fléchettes? They weren't really alive. Why were these Cartoons behaving with such studied malevolence? Why were they able to generate all the multitude of vocalizations that had been missing from earlier Cartoons? Still, the smell was wrong, the ship hadn't gotten that, not yet.

Jobs was relieved. The ship was still getting things wrong. That made it easier for him to remember that this was all nothing but force fields and matter generators and no doubt some wonderfully sophisticated programming.

What was the ship up to? What was this all about?

One thing was sure, the Cartoons were getting more aggressive. Closer. Louder. A solid wall of nightmares now, all around. Jobs and his friends and the alien were moving in a bubble now, surrounded, cut off, walking straight through some medieval madman's vision of hell.

They passed by a blue bird seated on a high golden throne. On its head it wore an iron cooking pot at a jaunty angle.

It was eating a man, the legs and rear still protruding. Small black birds were flying out of the man's rear end.

Jobs said, "What is that?"

Violet looked up, saw the eerie thing, and said, "Allegory."

"An allegory of what?" Jobs demanded. "An allegory about don't get eaten by a big huge blue bird or else crows will fly out of your butt?"

"I don't know," Violet admitted. "It meant something to someone once. Maybe."

"Or maybe your painter guy was just nuts," Jobs snapped.

"He's not *my* painter," Violet said wearily. "I'm not running this freak show. If I were running this freak show there'd be a hot bath somewhere."

The movement was sudden and swift. It would have been ludicrous if not so dangerous. Two ears, human ears, detached from any head, held together by a long spear stabbed through the upper lobe. The ears were twice man-height. And wedged between them was a knife, a knife big enough to carve up an elephant. The blade itself was ten feet long.

The knife-wielding ears were being pushed and shoved by a small army of starved, moaning men, enthusiastically whipped on by demons.

And now, accelerated by the constant cracks of demon whips, the knife was coming straight toward Jobs and his friends. There was no doubt in his mind that the ears meant to kill him. The horror was only heightened by his desire to giggle at the lunacy of it.

"This is nuts. This is insane," he said angrily. "Killer ears? Killer ears? Was this guy on drugs?"

At the same time, he backpedaled, carrying Billy and Mo'Steel back with him. But back where? A wall of demons awaited behind. The antlered deer stared blankly. The gray figure of death lowered its fleshless jaw in what might be a grin.

The knife swung down, like a falling tree, fast, not fast enough. It sliced into the dirt, the point swiping the air in front of Jobs's nose.

The blade popped up and the starved men shoved the absurd ear structure closer. They were determined now to stab, to stab the point right in Jobs's heart.

"No! No!"

Jobs dropped the stretcher. Billy rolled off.

The Blue Meanie raised one foreleg. There came the loud whirring sound and the cloud of fléchettes ripped into the ears, into the men pushing them, into the nearest demons. There was a cloud of red and brown. The ears looked as if they'd been chewed by a dog. They slid apart, the spear no longer linking them.

The gigantic knife toppled over and lay there.

"Thanks," Jobs said to the alien. Then he rolled Billy back onto the stretcher and touched the boy's head. "Thank you, Four Sacred Streams."

The alien's screen wrote, *Fléchette weapon now exhausted.*

The demon army fell back, hesitant but not in retreat. The deer tilted its head quizzically.

"How far to this node?" Jobs asked.

Not far.

"Why is Mother doing this?"

Mother is serving you.

"Well, tell her to stop!" Mo'Steel yelled.

"Can Mother be stopped? Can't we turn this off?"

The node must be destroyed.

Jobs kept his hand on Billy's head. He was shaky after the knife attack. Shaky after seeing Mo'Steel fall apart. He was tired and needed a rest. Mostly, he wanted to understand. If he could understand, he could fix. That was his lifelong belief: What he could understand, he could modify, reconfigure, repair. Render harmless or even useful.

"Aren't you the people who built this ship? Don't you control it?" Jobs demanded.

WE ARE NOT THE SHIPWRIGHTS. WE ARE THEIR CREATION. THEY ARE THE MAKERS. WE THOUGHT WE WERE THEIR CHILDREN, BUT WHEN THE AWAKENING CAME, WE SAW THAT WE WERE SLAVES OF THE MAKERS.

"Is this really the time?" Olga demanded. "Maybe we should conduct this interview some other time."

But Jobs was already asking his next question. "The Shipwrights? They made the ship and they made you? And then . . ."

Yes.

"They kicked you off the ship!" Jobs said as the pieces fell into place. "That's why you had to fight your way back on."

Yes.

"The Shipwrights made you to be slaves. You . . . that's it, isn't it? You're the repairmen. You're the software engineers."

We serve Mother.

"Mother is a computer."

MOTHER IS GREAT. MOTHER IS ALL. MOTHER IS OUR TRUE

MOTHER. MOTHER LOVES HER TRUE CHILDREN. BUT THE SHIPWRIGHTS POISONED MOTHER AGAINST US.

In an undertone Violet said, "These people never came up with their own Freud, did they?"

MOTHER'S TRUE CHILDREN LOVE HER. MOTHER'S TRUE CHILDREN HAVE RETURNED AFTER A LONG EXILE. MOTHER'S TRUE CHILDREN WILL RETURN MOTHER TO PERFECTION.

Olga shook her head. "The Shipwrights created the Meanies, the Meanies wanted freedom, so the Shipwrights made Mother expel them. Now the Meanies are back to retake Mother and earn back her love. Miss Blake is right: Everyone here needs therapy."

CHAPTER NINETEEN

"THE BABY IS HUNGRY."

"Riders!"

T.R. came racing in, breathless. "Riders! Many, many this time."

A second later, Tate confirmed. "They're coming up the ramp. The sun's starting to come up, you can see them. A lot. They're down in the town, coming this way."

T.R. nodded vigorously. His face was one big cringe, Yago thought. His fear was contagious.

"Check it out," Wylson told Yago.

Yago actually looked over his shoulder to see who Wylson might be talking to. "Me? What do you mean, check it out?"

"Go look. Get a count. I need to know how many there are."

Yago swallowed his first reaction, which was that Wylson didn't need to know anything because Wylson wasn't going to do anything. Instead he nodded in a businesslike fashion. "Okay."

He stepped outside and crossed the ramp. Tate was right, there was light. But not much. Just enough to make out the buildings below, and just enough to see the Riders. They were in the open belt between town and tower.

And Tate was right: There were a lot of them. Yago counted twenty-seven before he gave up, overwhelmed by hopelessness.

Maybe he should run, right now. By himself. 2Face had done it. She'd left with Edward. Of course they were probably both dead now, so maybe that wasn't the best example.

What chance did Yago have sticking with this crowd? Wylson play-acted at being in charge, but Tamara was the boss. They were in a war and Tamara was the only warrior.

"There's a lesson for you," Yago muttered to himself. "In a war the warrior rules."

He went back in, still unsure what to do. It came down to Tamara and the baby. Could they conceivably beat this small army of Riders? If they could, then Yago's future was with the group. If not . . .

2Face had been clever, maybe. Anyway, she had thwarted Yago's plans. For now.

"I count at least twenty-seven," Yago reported to Wylson, Burroway, and T.R.

A part of him was amused. The grown-ups — the department heads in Wylson's little fantasy world — tried to look wise and steady, but Burroway was sweating and T.R. had a death-mask smile going on.

Wylson was trying heroically to avoid looking at Tamara. The Marine squatted in a corner, leaned back against the stone wall, eyes closed, resting. The baby played with its toes, like any normal baby. Like any freakishly big, eyeless, normal baby who never pooped or ate or cried.

"Recommendations?" Wylson snapped, stalling for time.

"What?" Burroway demanded, alarmed.

"What recommendations do you have?" Wylson asked shrilly.

"Are you insane? They're coming," Burroway snapped.

"We have to run for it," T.R. said. "We have to run."

"Ask the sergeant," Burroway said, stabbing a finger toward Tamara. "Go to her! Ask her if she can save us."

He said it loudly enough for everyone in the

room to hear the edge of panic. The baby looked up from its toes and stared with its gaping sockets.

A small, ironic smile flitted across Tamara's face. She didn't move or open her eyes.

"That's your recommendation?" Wylson asked Burroway. "Fine. Implement that."

"You stupid, delusional idiot," Burroway raged suddenly, all restraint gone. "Shut up, you stupid woman! Stupid, stupid woman."

Wylson clenched her jaw and glared fiercely at Burroway. "You are endangering your position on this board."

"We have to stick together," T.R. said.

"Now you want to stick together," Shy Hwang sneered with a darting look at Yago.

"Someone figure out something, all right?" Anamull yelled, barging into the "meeting."

Tate went to Tamara and stood over her, hands on hips. Tate was African-American, short, decidedly feminine, the polar opposite of Tamara. She had a shaved head except for a spray of dreadlocks at the back, a knotted ponytail that hung to her midback.

Tate said, "Are you going to help us or not, Tamara? *Can* you help us?"

Everyone froze. Everyone waited. The vital question had at last been asked.

"Me?" Tamara unlimbered herself, stood up, and brushed at imaginary dust on her tattered uniform. She picked the baby up and settled him on her hip.

"There are almost thirty of them this time," Tate said, standing her ground. "Can you stop them?"

Tamara looked down at the baby and the baby slowly, lasciviously, licked its lips.

"The baby is hungry," Tamara said.

That non sequitur sustained the silence.

"Are you going to help us?" Tate asked again.

"The baby is hungry. The baby is too hungry for a fight right now."

"So feed it," Yago snapped impatiently.

Tamara's eyes flickered, looked down, almost as if embarrassed by what she had to say. Yago was sure he saw a look of pained incomprehension, quickly replaced by acceptance.

"The baby is hungry for . . . for meat. For fresh meat," Tamara said. "It doesn't matter who: Any one of you will do."

CHAPTER TWENTY

"I'D RATHER BE AT DISNEY WORLD."

Edward froze. 2Face was gone. He froze, stood still, as if his legs were turned to stone.

The monsters were behind him; all he had to do was turn around to see them. Monsters more horrible than anything from any nightmare.

When he was little he had dreamed of dinosaurs. His dreams had been jerky, sped-up movies of dinosaurs, Triceratops and Tyrannosaurus moving like claymation figures, only bigger, so big they could have stomped his room flat.

Sometimes he had dreamed of bogeymen, of all the creatures that populated his Tolkien and Rowling books. They danced around him, taunting him, taking his toys. Sometimes they would creep out of his dreams and hide in his bedroom closet. Once he saw goblins dancing atop his dresser, saw them as clearly as anything could be seen.

But this was different. These monsters made his stomach hurt. These monsters made him want to go in his pants. Even the ones that weren't ugly were horrible in a way that made his skin crawl over his bones.

And now he was alone with them.

They were coming closer. Edging around him. One poked him and he yelled, "Cut it out!"

He turned slowly, slowly, and tears spilled down his cheeks. He faced the monsters. He was sobbing, his chin quivering, his throat seizing.

"Leave me alone," he begged.

One of the demons, a creature with a cat's face and a frog's body, whipped out a two-foot-long tongue and slurped Edward's face. The demons all laughed at that. The red one danced jigs.

A troll woman — that's what Edward thought it was, anyway — came waddling up. She was fat and blue and short. She carried a cast-iron pot filled with some black liquid that steamed and popped.

The troll woman set the pot down and with a rush two demons seized Edward's arms and held him tight. They lifted him up off his feet and carried him toward the pot.

"No! No! No!"

The demons just laughed and lifted him high. He

could feel the heat from the pot; it was burning his legs and bottom as he screamed and writhed away from it.

"Yaaaaahhhh!"

A spear erupted from the chest of one of the demons. It stuck out almost a foot, stuck straight out from where his heart should be.

"Aaaahhhh!" 2Face yelled and thrust with all her might, leaning all her weight into the spear, which pushed on through the first demon and into the second.

The demons released their hold, Edward fell, grabbing onto the spear, scrabbled wildly trying to hold on. If he slipped he would be in the pot.

2Face lunged at him, pushed him hard so that he fell backward, off the spear, onto the ground.

He jumped up and 2Face was there, grabbing his arm and pulling him with her.

The demon mob seemed startled by this new turn of events. The two skewered monsters tried ineffectually to remove the spear that bound them together.

Edward and 2Face ran, out onto the ramp, out into gray dawn, out into a cold slap of air.

"Sorry I ran away. I was scared," 2Face gasped.

"I messed my pants," Edward moaned.

"Yeah? Well, you were entitled, kid."

"Where are we going? Are we going to find my brother?"

"How about we just put some distance between us and those Halloween characters back there?"

"Okay."

"Let me just say this, if this whole ship really is some kind of amusement park or whatever, it is for some sick, messed-up people. Tell you one thing, Edward: I'd rather be at Disney World."

CHAPTER TWENTY-ONE

"I THINK THEIR BOSS IS COMING."

"Stay close, stay tight," Mo'Steel said. "Mom? You okay?"

"I'm fine," Olga said through gritted teeth.

"I think maybe I better drop back and see if I can keep these guys off us," Mo'Steel said. "Mom, you better take the stretcher here."

"What can you do?" Olga wondered. "We have no weapons and the alien says he's out of flé-chettes."

"I can maybe scare them a little," Mo'Steel said, not believing it for a moment. But he'd disgraced himself in his own eyes. He'd bunnied. Things got a little woolly and he'd lost it.

Jobs had been right all along: Nothing real here. Yes, real in that the monsters were not like some kind of projection or whatever; they were flesh and bone or something material, anyway. And when they poked you with a sharp stick it hurt.

But they weren't real demons. Maybe that painter a long time ago had some kind of vision, maybe, but this was just like a kind of movie or whatever of that. A computer game. That's what it was.

Too bad Mo'Steel had never liked computer games. He didn't know how to play. He'd always liked reality. And now reality was a computer game.

"Mom, you take Billy. I'm going to drop back and give these creeps something to think about."

Olga reluctantly took the stretcher. Mo'Steel spared a moment for a reassuring look. "Hey, it's me, Mom. You know nothing can kill me."

His mother's face was gray with worry.

"What are you doing, Mo?" Jobs demanded.

Mo'Steel turned and crossed the five feet to the nearest demon in a matter of seconds. It was a peculiar mix of huge fish and rat walking on two heavily booted feet. On its back was a man's helmeted head.

"How about this?" Mo'Steel said. He jumped up and kicked the helmeted head. It toppled off the rat-fish and ran off on twisted arms.

"Not all that tough, huh?" Mo'Steel crowed.

A swollen golden monkey was next. Mo'Steel slapped him across his monkey face.

"Yeah! Bring it to me," he yelled at the demon. "Back up is what I'm saying. You're crowding us. Back up or I'll have to do some more butt-kicking."

Over his shoulder he saw one of the monsters dart in and stab his mother in the side with a knife. Olga screamed and dropped the stretcher.

"Mom!"

Suddenly a shriveled, gray-skinned female creature swung at Mo'Steel with a sword as long as her own body.

The blade sliced across his chest, cut through the rotted clothing, and cut into the flesh.

Mo'Steel yelped in pain and surprise. The little demon giggled and ran. Mo'Steel dove after her, grabbed her by the neck, twisted her around, and yanked the sword from her bony hand.

A dozen demons piled onto him and he was smothered by flesh — human, animal, and none-of-the-above.

Now the pain and fear combined to generate a rage like nothing Mo'Steel had ever felt in his easy-going life. His mind went black. He seemed to be staring through a veil of blood. Fear was gone, nothing but rage, screaming fury.

"You want to hurt my mom!" he screamed again and again, as his fists punched and legs kicked at anything within reach. He stabbed blindly with the sword, unable to swing because there was no room, no room for anything but stabbing and kicking and screaming into the reeking, horrible faces pressed in all around him.

All at once he rolled free, gasping for breath, each breath causing a red-hot stab of pain from his chest wound. The muscles of his chest felt like they were burning.

His head was swimming. He saw his mother on her knees, surrounded by demons. Jobs was waving something and yelling in a shrill voice. Billy Weir had rolled into the dirt, facedown in filth. Violet was shrieking, flailing away at a pair of rats as big as she was.

It had all happened in a heartbeat.

Mo'Steel staggered to his feet, ran, jumped feet-first into one of the demons tormenting his mother, and knocked the creature sprawling.

They had Violet down on the ground, spread-eagled, one on each hand, each foot. A crone with the legs of a frog was holding a long, sharp pole. She was going to impale Violet. A huge swollen bird played its horn of a beak, wild, discordant music.

Violet was screaming, screaming, screaming, like an ambulance siren.

Mo'Steel swung his sword and sliced the head from the demon he'd knocked over. He ran full tilt at the frog-woman and hacked at her neck. He caught her in the hump of her back and the blade stuck. The frog-woman barely seemed to notice. She shrugged and steadied the aim of her stick. She drew back and thrust as Mo'Steel yanked ineffectually at the sword blade.

The Blue Meanie stepped between the crone and Violet. With one leg he snapped the sharpened pole. He whirled with impressive speed and slapped the crone with a hind leg. The crone flew ten feet and crashed into the mass of demons.

The letters on the Meanie's chest read: *MUST DESTROY THE NODE.*

"Where?" Mo'Steel rasped.

The Meanie understood the question without Billy's interpretation. It pointed. *There.*

Mo'Steel glanced and saw a forge. The coals glowed yellow and red.

"That?"

THE NODE.

Something hit Mo'Steel from behind. He staggered, blind and whirling. He fell hard. His head was swimming. He saw dream shapes: demons and monsters and his friends. His mother.

He tried to get up, collapsed, tried again, and gained his feet woozily. He was beyond rational thought now, his brain too rattled to think clearly. He kicked a monster in the leg and laughed when it fell. He bumped into another and toppled it.

He fell again, headlong, too dizzy. He fell beside Billy Weir. Billy's face was in the dirt; he was breathing worm-wiggly mud. Mo'Steel gently pushed Billy's head, freeing his mouth and nose.

"Could use some help here, 'migo," he said to the blank eyes.

"Mo! Mo! Are you okay? Can you hear me?"

Mo'Steel rolled onto his back and saw Jobs's face looking down at him. Mo'Steel smiled sweetly. "Hey, Duck."

"Oh, man, Mo, I thought you were dead."

"Me? Nah, man. When I die I won't be coming here."

Slowly his head cleared. He got to his knees and threw up. He felt weak all over, shaky. He felt gingerly for the lump at the back of his head. It wasn't big, not yet anyway, though he suspected it would be in time. He'd had concussions before: He knew what they felt like.

"My mom?"

"She's okay," Jobs said. "But we have to move. We have to move. Something is coming."

Even in his near delirium Mo'Steel didn't like the look on Jobs's face. "What's coming?"

"I think it's why the demons backed off."

"Oh, man."

"I think their boss is coming."

CHAPTER TWENTY-TWO

"FEED A FREAK TO THE FREAK."

Yago was ready for most anything that would allow him to seize power. He was not sure he was ready to designate a victim to be fed to the baby.

"What?" he said.

Tamara shrugged. "The baby is hungry."

"So feed it," Wylson said.

Tamara looked embarrassed. "It won't feed that way. It doesn't want milk. I've tried."

"Well, try again," Yago snapped.

The baby leered at him and made little popping sounds with its mouth. It had a mouth full of teeth.

"There are limits," T.R. said, as though he wasn't sure he believed it.

"The Riders are coming," Burroway snapped.

"Are you volunteering?" Wylson yelled, turning angrily on him.

"I hardly think I should be the one to . . . to be

sacrificed," Burroway said. "I have knowledge and skills that are vital to the . . . to . . . to this mission," he ended lamely.

"No, no, no," Yago said. "We go this way this time, it'll be eating us one after another."

The baby laughed as if confirming this.

"They're on the ramp!" a voice cried from outside. "The Riders are on the ramp!"

"They'll be here in a few minutes," Burroway said. "We have to do something."

"Excuse us, would you, Tamara?" Wylson said with exaggerated politeness.

Wylson, Yago, Burroway, and T.R. huddled and spoke in frantic whispers.

"It's some kind of sick game," Yago said. "I don't think they mean it. The baby is just —"

"The needs of the many outweigh the needs of —"

"How would we decide who is —"

"Not one of us, we're all needed!"

Yago saw a blur of movement, a rush of people backing away. 2Face and Edward came racing through the arch.

"Do you people know there are Riders coming?" 2Face demanded.

"Her," Yago hissed. "Feed a freak to the freak."

"It's the only way," Burroway said. "It's terrible, but we can't sacrifice everyone for the sake of one life."

"Burroway is right," Yago said quickly. "I didn't want it to be, but it is the right thing, Wylson, we have to. No choice."

Wylson gulped. She shook her head. "No. I'll talk to Tamara."

"No time!" T.R. hissed. He grabbed Wylson's arm.

She shook loose, stared at him like she was seeing a monster, and stalked off.

"She'll come around," Yago said. "We have to be ready."

"What do you mean?" Burroway asked, frowning.

"I mean, we need to have 2Face ready to be served up. Let me get D-Caf and Anamull. They'll help."

"Ask me, it ought to be D-Caf we give her," Burroway grumbled. "He's the killer."

Yago knew Burroway would do nothing more, but it gave him an idea. He grabbed D-Caf. "You know what's going on?"

D-Caf nodded fearfully.

"They all wanted it to be you, Twitch. They all

said we should feed you to the baby. I stopped them. You remember that, someday. You remember you're alive because of me."

D-Caf swallowed hard and nodded, still fearful.

"It's going to be 2Face," Yago said grimly. "Go get Anamull. Keep your mouths shut, both of you. But I want you both near 2Face, you got me? When I give the word, you guys grab her, knock her out or something."

D-Caf ran off and Yago fought down the queasiness in his stomach. This was *way* off the charts. This wasn't politics, this wasn't anything but messed up and wrong.

Still, it was working out for him. He would get rid of 2Face and make D-Caf and Anamull his guilty accomplices. He'd own D-Caf from here on in, and Anamull, too. Maybe he should see who else he could use to his advantage.

He caught sight of Wylson arguing with Tamara. Wylson's hands were waving, chopping the air. Tamara slouched, bored, while the baby seemed to stare at Wylson's throat.

Sick. All of it sick. But this was a sick place and a man had to do what a man had to do to make it. 2Face's return had been like a gift. She was already an outsider. After all, hadn't she abandoned everyone and run off with Edward? She'd already been a traitor.

He should remind everyone of that. No one would stop to wonder why she'd run off to begin with.

D-Caf, with Anamull in tow, lurked within arm's reach of her. *It was almost over for the freak,* Yago thought. *Almost over and she doesn't even know it.*

CHAPTER TWENTY-THREE

"SING TO MY PEOPLE OF MY DEATH."

As artwork, Satan didn't impress Violet very much. Bosch had used all his imagination to invent every conceivable variation on the creepy, startling, disturbingly funny demons and denizens of this hell that when it came time to reveal the demon of all demons, the ultimate evil, he had little new.

Not that the oversized monstrosity of whipping tail and blazing eyes of fire wasn't enough to make the flesh creep. But aside from the deference paid to it by the other demons, it seemed like nothing special.

On the other hand, the monster seemed to be rallying his troops to a final, all-out assault on the interlopers.

"Is that supposed to be Satan? I thought he'd be redder," Mo'Steel said. "I thought red."

Violet was relieved that Mo'Steel had, at least for

the moment, conquered his fear. He was not the type of male Violet preferred, but he was strong and brave and those two attributes were paramount in this place.

"The Meanie's saying something," Jobs said. "Look."

THE NODE. TIME IS SHORT.

The alien pointed with his one remaining facial tentacle. He pointed at the blasted, burned-out, half-collapsed building where the demonic Vulcan was feeding another of the damned into the roaring flames.

Four Sacred Streams started to move more quickly, impatient. Violet and the others fell into step behind him, glad to have anyone to follow.

Satan — there was no other way to think of him — moved on spindly rat legs to cut them off. His minions came at a rush to join him. Demons who had been busy torturing the doomed now dropped what they were doing and came at a run or a crawl or a scurry.

"The ship has figured it out," Jobs yelled above the rising cries of demonic alarm. "It knows we're after the node!"

Even as he spoke, an arrow flew, a bolt from a crossbow, and struck in one of the stretcher poles.

Four Sacred Streams broke into a run. It was easy enough now to see that it was hampered by the damaged armor. It was meant to fly and no longer could. And Violet was sure it was meant to be able to run more quickly and evenly than this. The alien barely kept pace with the running humans.

Violet stumbled over broken stony ground, running despite the burning in her chest. She cursed the long dress and useless shoes that stabbed her ankles with each step.

"Jane Austen, meet Dante," she muttered, giggling insanely at the witticism, anything to keep from crying and collapsing.

Something leaped at her from the side. She felt claws rip at her, tearing at her hair. She screamed and the demon fell away and she forgot the pain in her feet and hand and ran in all-out panic.

A thing made of amputated body parts rushed at her. Faces were thrust close to her from all around, hands and claws grabbed, mouths snapped, all in a swirl, all around, touching her, grabbing, pushing, trying to trip.

She ran, heedless, pushing back, slapping wildly, kicking awkwardly.

She ran straight into an open pit filled with tar.

Faces contorted in pain and disbelief stared up at her. She fell in, sank into the hot tar, felt it against her flesh, felt it clog her clothing.

She screamed in shock and heard her scream echoed from a disembodied head floating beside her. She slapped her hands on the edge of the pit and tried to haul herself up, but the pull of the tar was too strong. Like a fly trying to climb out of cold molasses.

She sagged, held on with her elbows. She was crying freely now, tears blurring everything into a crazy carnival of fantastic faces and weird, impossible forms.

She slipped and held her head free only by virtue of sticking her arms straight out in front of her. She was holding on by her armpits as the faces of the tormented souls bobbed around her, rising to scream, sliding down with a gurgle.

A bird-man, a bird with an impossibly long, razor-sharp beak walking erect on booted feet pecked at her arms.

"No!" she cried. "Leave me alone. Leave me alone. Please, please, please just leave me alone."

A gray-skinned gargoyle with a hideous fright-mask grin laughed at her, laughed in her face and began to pry her fingers up from the ground. She slipped farther.

"No, no, no. Please don't hurt me. Please stop. Please."

Violet lost her hold and slid backward, inexorably sucked into the pit. She saw demons dancing jigs around the edge of the pit and then her face slid under the tar.

"Where's Miss Blake?" Jobs cried. He looked but there was nothing to see, nothing but the mob of taunting demons, the foul fantasy creatures all around.

One stabbed at him with a short spear and he felt a jolt of pain in his behind. He clapped a hand on the wound and dropped the stretcher.

He felt the spear still protruding and with a desperate cry pulled it free. He swung the spear awkwardly and hit nothing. He searched for the stretcher but somehow he had been swept past it. The tide of evil creatures hid everyone and everything from sight.

"Mo!" he yelled. "Mo! Mo!"

A stunning blow caught him from behind and he fell hard, facedown. The wind was gone from his lungs. Hands were everywhere, holding him, lifting him up. He cried out as he rose, carried aloft like some kind of prize.

"Mo! Help me! Help me!"

Demons carried him high, then turned him over, facedown. Facedown they stretched him, pulling at his legs and arms, pulling him till he thought he might be torn apart. They carried him at a run and then Jobs saw what they planned.

The knife's blade was turned up, the knife horizontal, four feet off the ground. It was ten feet long.

They carried Jobs till he was suspended directly over the knife, lengthwise, so that dropping him would slice him in half.

Jobs wanted to scream but his voice was gone. He tried but no sound emerged.

The demons did not drop him. They lowered him with extravagant care and gently laid him on the knife's edge. He lay there with hands hanging, legs hanging, the blade creasing his belly and chest and lips and nose.

One move and he would die. One slight increase in pressure and the blade would cut him.

And now the demons turned a crank that rattled and creaked and slowly raised the knife point high. Jobs was facing downhill and in a few eternal seconds he would begin to slide down the length of the knife blade.

Mo'Steel was alone, no Jobs, his mother gone, surrounded and attacked from all sides, cut and bruised and slashed. He glimpsed Four Sacred Streams, the only familiar sight in a landscape of evil.

He heard Jobs's scream.

"Jobs!' he yelled. But he couldn't see his friend. Could do nothing at all, nothing but slap aside a spear thrust and keep running after the Blue Meanie.

The alien was under sustained attack, but the spears did not penetrate his armor, and the claws that snatched at him slid off the deep blue Mylar, unable to gain a hold.

The Blue Meanie pressed forward, pushing now against the sheer physical weight of a howling mob. Pushing his low-slung head into the belly of the devil himself.

Mo'Steel ripped a spear from a demon's hand and threw it. Threw it straight at the eyes that glowed bright red from beneath a turban.

The spear hit the devil a glancing blow, and in return, for taking his attention away from self-defense, Mo'Steel was punished with a raking, skin-scoring slash from a talon like a hawk's.

The Meanie pushed on and Mo'Steel could do nothing but follow, nothing but try and keep going forward. Where was his mother? His best friend?

The Blue Meanie stopped, unable to go any farther.

He twisted around and faced Mo'Steel. There were words scrolling across his chest. Mo'Steel could barely make sense of them. Nonsense words.

SING TO MY PEOPLE OF MY DEATH.

"What?"

The blow that knocked Mo'Steel down made his ears ring. He felt himself flying, flying low, with his face just above the ground.

A fire. He could feel its heat.

A huge round pan, sizzling hot, held over the fire by a reptilian crone.

The demons swung him back, forth, back, building up momentum, and then threw him, tumbling, through the air.

CHAPTER TWENTY-FOUR

"MMM, BABY WANT SOME NUM NUM."

2Face felt as much as saw the presence of Anamull and D-Caf. She knew they were watching her. She knew they were tensed, ready to spring, waiting for a signal.

But she didn't know why until her father came to her and embraced her awkwardly.

"I'm glad you're back," Shy Hwang said. "But this may be a bad time."

"It's always a bad time now," she answered warily.

"It's the baby," he said with a significant look.

"What about the baby?"

"It's hungry. It wants to eat. And if we don't feed it, then Tamara won't fight the Riders, and they're coming, a lot this time."

"So feed it." She searched his face for some deeper meaning. He looked away.

2Face shook him but he didn't say anything. She

looked up, mystified, and saw Yago. Yago didn't look happy. He looked haunted, ragged. He met her eyes and then shifted focus to just past her. He nodded.

Anamull grabbed her upper arm in an iron grip. He still had his dagger. He put the tip near her throat.

"No!" Shy Hwang cried. "No, you can't do this."

D-Caf said, "Yago said. Yago said." Tentatively he grabbed 2Face's free arm.

"This is wrong. You can't do this!" Shy yelled, but he didn't move. "Not my daughter, too. I've already lost my wife. No!"

"Move," Anamull whispered in 2Face's ear.

She felt herself propelled forward, passing faces that first looked in horror and then turned away.

"What are you doing?" she demanded and tried to shake free.

"Baby hungry," Anamull said with an idiot giggle.

"It has to be someone," D-Caf said, arguing with himself. "And she did leave. She ran off. I mean, that's like you abandoned us. Has to be someone."

"And she's already half-cooked," Anamull said and exploded in laughter.

2Face's heart was in her throat. She saw Burroway, his face hard, eyes meeting hers then going vacant.

"What is going on here?" 2Face cried. She saw Tamara in the corner. Saw Wylson with her back to Tamara. The baby, perched on Tamara's hip.

"No," 2Face whispered.

"Baby hungry," Anamull said in his heavy parody of baby talk. "Mmm, baby want some num num."

Yago loomed before her. "I really am sorry about this. I doubt you'll believe me, but I am sorry. There's no other way."

"The needs of the many outweigh the needs of the one," T.R. intoned.

"We're doing this?" Yago asked Wylson.

"We're trying to survive," Wylson said. Her eyes were wide, her mouth pulled back in a parody of a smile. A fear smile, like a terrified dog.

"Give the word, then," Yago said softly.

"We all know what we're doing," Wylson said evasively.

Yago nodded. "But you're the boss, right?"

"We all agreed," Wylson said. "And you said it should be 2Face."

Tate thrust in between them. "This is wrong, you cowards. Let's fight the Riders ourselves. This is wrong, you can't do this."

"You go fight the Riders," Yago snapped. "Or maybe you want to trade places with 2Face?"

"We're in a new place, we're all that's left of the human race, you can't do this!" Tate cried.

"Not volunteering, huh?" Yago nodded to Anamull. "Okay, to the baby."

2Face began kicking, dragging her heels, squirming. But D-Caf tightened his grip and Anamull was powerful. Her mind was reeling, eyes swimming, turning everything bright and blurry.

"You can't do this!" she cried.

"Guess we can," Yago said calmly. "It's about survival. Not my idea."

"No, you just named the victim," 2Face spat.

Yago nodded thoughtfully. "Yes, I did."

"What do you think you get by killing me?" 2Face asked desperately.

Yago said nothing. She dug in her heels and cursed but she kept moving toward Tamara and the baby. The baby clapped its hands happily.

From far off, 2Face heard Tate still shouting, demanding others act, demanding that someone show some spine.

"Once I'm gone you'll have no scapegoat," 2Face pleaded desperately.

"I'll find someone."

"Or someone will find you, Yago. You think you're safe? You're not killing me because I'm weak, you're killing me because you know I'm dangerous — don't you think someone will feel the same about you?"

Yago's cat-DNA-enhanced eyes flickered.

"Eliminate competition, that's the game, right? Get rid of anyone who might stand in your way, right? Whose way do *you* stand in, Yago?" She was talking a mile a minute, still kicking and squirming but thinking and rattling out the words.

"Wylson, Yago. You don't think she has you in mind for the next time? She's smarter than you are, Yago; she's going to blame you for this, pin this on you and then sacrifice you the next time — you'll never be the boss till she's gone and you're killing the wrong person and she'll get you because she's smarter and stronger and more focused and she's not stupid enough to let some stupid blow-off force her hand, not Wylson, she'll —"

She stopped talking. Yago had motioned Anamull and D-Caf to stop.

Yago stepped close. Behind him 2Face could see the backs of all who had turned away.

"Look behind you, Yago," 2Face whispered harshly. "Everyone turned away. They're making you carry the weight. You'll be blamed for murder. You'll be the scapegoat. That makes you next on the baby's menu."

Yago glanced back, stared, slowly turned back to 2Face, eyes mean, face pinched. "You have a suggestion?" he asked.

"You want to be boss?" 2Face said. "Wylson is boss now. As long as she's around, she's boss and you're not."

Their eyes met and locked.

"If I turn against her I'm still the scapegoat, I'm still the killer," Yago said.

"I'll do it," 2Face said. "Get her over here. Let me get away for just a minute, I'll take care of it."

Yago's eyebrows shot up. "You'll take her down?"

"I'll knock her out. If she's unconscious, who's going to argue with her being the sacrifice? No one likes her. And the blame will be on me, so I won't be a threat to your being in charge."

"You're a cold little lizard, aren't you?" Yago said, nodding in admiration.

Then, in a loud voice, he said, "Wylson! You're the boss. If you want this done, you come over and do it in person."

Yago smiled at 2Face. "Well, well," he said, "we're two of a kind."

CHAPTER TWENTY-FIVE

"DON'T TELL ME YOU ENJOYED ALL THAT."

Violet flailed, legs kicked, arms waved, slowly, slowly, sinking, down and down, darkness, mouth smothered, eyes blind, ears full of grunted screams, sank and needed to breathe. To breathe. Lungs on fire . . .

Olga was strapped tight to a long pole, bound with rawhide strips, arms behind her. And now the demons carried the pole to the fire, walked through the fire unharmed themselves, and laid the ends of the pole into the forked uprights. She was on a spit, hanging facedown above a fire. Waves of heat, searing, impossible heat burned her eyebrows and eyelashes and crinkled her hair. She breathed in the stink of her own burning hair and knew she would soon hear the crisping of her own skin.

*   *   *

Jobs pressed his palms against the blade and pushed upward, trying to raise his weight off that fatal edge. But as he levered himself up he felt the blade begin to slice into him. He lowered himself back down, sobbing. He had to keep his weight perfectly still, perfectly balanced; one move, one shift, so much as a vibration and the blade would begin slicing and then his weight and his every movement would work the blade farther and farther into him. He couldn't slide down, couldn't slide, no no no no, they were raising the blade higher, palms pressed hard, had to hold on, if he slipped along the blade, if he let go, if his sweating palms slipped . . .

Mo'Steel felt himself flying. Flashed on the fire, the pan, the demons cackling happily. He yanked his legs under him. No way to land on his feet, had to be knees, in and out, hard but not impossible. He landed on his knees, absorbed the shock into his hips, held his hands back so as not to burn them, and sprang up and away like a scared grasshopper. Had to keep the momentum, had to use the speed, had to work with Mother G.

He went butt-over and landed on his back with his head in the fire. He used the very last of his momentum and all his strength, flung himself forward and onto his face, out of the fire.

There was a roar of concern from the disappointed demons. They rushed at him and now he had no momentum, no strength, and no hope. They lifted him, faceup, held him and this time readied to lay him in the pan and hold him there till he was too far gone ever to jump again.

Mo'Steel bellowed in rage and twisted his head up to spit fury at his tormentors.

He saw the Blue Meanie, far away now, ascending the ruined wall of the node. Climbing slowly as the demons piled on him.

"Help!" Mo'Steel screamed.

But the alien was past helping anyone.

"Can't you handle this yourself, Yago?" Wylson snapped savagely.

"You're the boss," Yago said with an insolent shrug.

"What good are you!" Wylson raged. "This is your kind of thing, isn't it?"

Yago moved away, knowing Wylson would turn to face him, knowing she would expose her back to 2Face.

"You know —" Yago began to say.

Anamull released 2Face. 2Face clasped her

hands together, raised them over her head, and brought them down with all her strength on the back of Wylson's neck.

Wylson staggered forward.

2Face hit her again and Wylson fell flat.

"What are you doing, 2Face?" Yago yelled in a believable parody of surprise and outrage. "I think you may have killed her!"

"Riders are here!" Tate screamed from the archway.

2Face played out her role. "Wylson's out. She's food. You want me, I'll fight and it'll take time."

"She's right," Yago wailed. "Anyway, Wylson would understand."

2Face bent over and grabbed Wylson's ankle. She dragged the softly moaning woman toward Tamara and the baby.

Tamara looked upset, but the baby was giggling, almost hysterically.

2Face fell on her rear as she lost her hold on Wylson, and now Tamara put the baby down beside the half-conscious businesswoman.

"The Riders!" Yago gasped at Tamara.

"A deal's a deal," Tamara agreed.

The baby, with surprisingly strong hands, gripped Wylson's ankle.

* * *

The Blue Meanie cross-cut the power lines, sequenced the surge for maximum overload. The armor was almost out of power. It was the only way, and still it might not work.

Mother must be saved from herself. The node must be destroyed. It was the only way: Mother really needed her scheduled maintenance.

But it was a pity. So long in exile, so many generations. Four Sacred Streams had been privileged to return at last to the Sacred Mother of his people. To return, but never to enjoy Mother's love in a peaceful world.

Three seconds. Two.

The armor blew apart and Four Sacred Streams died instantly.

Violet knew she was dying, knew it and bitterly resented it. Smothering to death. Smothering, unable to resist breathing, her conscious mind no longer in control, breathing in the tar. It filled her mouth and began to surge down her throat.

She gagged, a last reflex.

And then, she was gagging on water.

Water!

She opened her eyes; she was in water — was she crazy, had she lost her mind? Was this death?

She waved her hands and met only moderate resistance. They moved! Her arms moved! No sticky tar, water. She was rising, slowly, hampered by her dress, slowly through the water.

Her head emerged. She could breathe!

"Finally," she gasped. "A bath."

This time the Riders did not pause to play games with Tamara; they came swooping up the ramp, six abreast, weapons at the ready, determined.

No more single combat. No more ritual. They knew what she was now — what the baby was, in any case — and they were afraid.

Tamara glanced back through the arch. Wylson was struggling to regain consciousness. 2Face stood over her, harsh, determined. Yago watched in fascination. The baby grinned at Tamara.

A glance was all Tamara could spare. The Riders wouldn't slow or stop, they would try to ride right over her, trap her between the first and second ranks of warriors, and finish her off with a 360-degree attack.

And they might well succeed.

Tamara had taken two boomerangs, three

spears, and a long scimitar from her earlier opponents. The weapons were draped around her body or lying nearby, within easy reach.

She lifted a boomerang and held it between thumb and forefinger. She took careful aim and threw it with all her unnatural strength.

The boomerang was not meant to kill on the first pass, or even on the return flight. It was aimed to cripple — a very un-Riderlike move, one they would not expect.

The boomerang hit the lead warrior's left legs and sliced them neatly in half. The warrior toppled into the Rider to his left and sent that warrior's board careening farther into the outermost Rider.

The three of them collided and tumbled.

"Too close," Tamara commented to no one. "They should have learned to keep an interval."

The three Riders still standing in the front row swerved. They did not fall, but neither did they keep their aim true. They swooped past Tamara, revealing the second line.

Six spears flew.

Tamara dropped to the ground and suddenly there was no ground.

She, the baby, the Riders, the others inside the tower that no longer existed all fell through the air.

* * *

Mo'Steel landed in a red-hot frying pan that was no longer there. He was wet!

Underwater?

He twisted, fast as a cat, and kicked hard for the surface. Only, he was disoriented. He hit bottom. It knocked the air from his lungs and water filled his mouth.

Turn around, Mo, he told himself. *Turn around.*

The water was no more than a few feet deep. He swarmed up to the surface and shot up and halfway out of the water like a dolphin.

He heard distant splashes. He twisted wildly, looking for others, looking for something to make sense of this madness.

The Tower of Babel and everything in it was gone. He was treading water in the middle of what could only be some sort of marsh. The water was warm and still and opaque with silt or microscopic life, or who knew what?

He saw something bobbing nearby and swam toward it. It was Billy Weir, lying faceup, rigid, floating too high in the water for it to be normal. Floating like a cork.

Mo'Steel wiped the water out of his eyes and cradled Billy's head unnecessarily. He could see his mother and Miss Blake together and felt a wave of relief.

Jobs was not far away, walking more than swimming. Mo'Steel put his legs down and realized that the water now was no more than four feet deep.

"What's up, Duck?" Mo'Steel asked his friend.

Jobs shook his head and let out a long, slow sigh. "Just one thing, Mo: Don't tell me you enjoyed all that. You're my friend, I love you like a brother, just don't tell me you enjoyed all that."

"No, no, man." Mo'Steel shook his head emphatically. "I'm cut, I'm bruised, I'm burned. My head's not right, still." Then, in a thoughtful tone, "Although . . ."

"Don't you 'although' me. I've been stabbed in the butt."

"I'm just saying . . ."

Violet and Olga slogged over to them. They looked wet and bedraggled. But Violet at least was smiling a survivor's smile: shocked and dazed and amazed to be alive.

"Hi, Mom. Hi, Miss Blake. So, Miss Blake, what crazy artscape is this?" Mo'Steel asked and swept his arm around at the marsh.

The light was dim, hazy, as if the air was full of smoke or steam, though no one was coughing and the air was cool. The water was dotted with low-lying islets, none seeming to be more than a few hundred feet long. There were trees of a sort, with slender, pliant trunks that waved in exaggerated response to even the breath of a breeze.

"I don't know," Violet said. "I don't . . . It's not like anything, really. Nothing I can place, anyway."

"Default," Jobs said.

"What?"

"The Meanie blew up the node. The ship isn't creating an environment anymore. I think this is the default setting. It's like a screen saver. I think this is what the place is like when the ship isn't actively creating an environment."

"This water isn't cold, but we still need a boat, 'migo," Mo'Steel said.

Jobs shook his head. "No, a hoverboard would be better. That's what it is, you know, that's what it's about."

"What what's about?" Violet asked.

"This is why the Riders are trying to kill us. This is the default setting. This is where they live, their country. This is their environment, except that Mother has changed it all — because of us."

"I thought the Blue Meanies were the ones who owned or whatever, who inhabited this place," Olga said.

"Yeah," Jobs agreed. "But the Meanies have been away for a long time. The Riders, the Blue Meanies, and us now. It's a three-way contest for control of Mother. And Mother . . . well, like Four Sacred Streams said: Mother is confused."

"Maybe we should have just stayed on Earth," Mo'Steel said. "You take it all together, Duck, and maybe it would have been easier just to get hit on the head by an asteroid."

Jobs nodded and sighed. He was glad to be out of the tower. But this landscape wasn't exactly inviting. "My butt hurts."

"My finger hurts," Violet said.

"My side," Olga muttered, "hurts pretty bad."

"My everything," Mo'Steel said. Then his tone shifted. "On the other hand, we escaped from hell, right? How much worse a mess can Mother come up with?"

"A malfunctioning alien supercomputer loaded with all the horrors the human mind has ever conjured up?" Jobs said. "We don't want to know what else it can come up with. Let's go find the others. Maybe they had an easier time."

2Face had fallen like the others when the tower simply ceased to exist. She had fallen and splashed in the water and hit the bottom. She'd been stunned silly and barely crawled her way back to the surface.

Now she dog-paddled in a place where the water was too deep to stand.

There was a low island nearby; she could see dim lights through the gloom. And she could hear the noises of the Riders. Celebrating, maybe. Or preparing for renewed battle.

And she could see some of the others, the other Remnants, huddling together, wandering, swimming, standing.

She should join them. She had no choice, really. No choice. Nowhere else to go.

Her hands were bruised from hitting Wylson.

"Did what you had to do," she told herself. "You just did what you had to do."

K.A. APPLEGATE

REMNANTS™

Nowhere Land

"THE SUN RISES, AND WITH IT, HOPE."

Yago saw them coming: Jobs, his creepy mutant brother, his monkey-boy pal, Mo'Steel's mother, the lovely and definitely timeworthy Miss Blake, Billy Weird, and, of course, 2Face.

What to do now? That was the question. What to do, and who to do it to.

How to play it? Like he and 2Face were allies? Or should he try to switch back to Wylson? And what about his two toadies, D-Caf and Anamull?

Hard to know how it was all going to play out.

Mostly, Yago realized, he was wet.

"This is so weird," D-Caf said.

"You think?" Yago said with nasty sarcasm.

"The sun is coming up," D-Caf offered helpfully.

"Yes. The sun rises, and with it, hope. Hope for a better world. Hope for peace and love and uncomplicated happiness."

"Really?" D-Caf asked.

Yago glared at him. "Are you the dumbest human being left alive? We're up to our armpits in water. We're lost and probably surrounded by Riders. We have a leader who thinks she's running a business seminar, and our only fighter is an alien baby who likes meat. We have no food, no weapons . . ."

D-Caf grinned and raised something from below the surface of the water. "I have a weapon. Do you want it?"

Yago stared. A Rider boomerang. It was a cruel-looking thing, toothed blades all along one edge.

"When everything was dissolving and right before we fell, I picked it up," D-Caf explained.

"Give it here," Yago said, but without any great pleasure. He wasn't a weapons person. He had no clue how to throw the thing. In fact it seemed likely he'd end up cutting off a few of his own fingers.

On the other hand, it was probably a good thing to —

"Aaahhh! Aaaahhhh!"

A cry of shrill panic.

Yago's head snapped around, looking for the

cause. It was Roger Dodger, a kid, going wild, slapping at the water and looking like he wanted to jump out of it.

The kid went still. He said, "I . . . I felt something."

"You nearly gave me a stroke," Burroway snapped.

"Maybe it wasn't anything," Roger Dodger said doubtfully.

Then Burroway shrieked. "Something bit me! It's in the water, something in the water bit me."

There was a pause, everyone waiting, staring, all conversation done for now. And then it was Shy Hwang yelping and holding up a bloody arm with something still attached, something squirmy and muscular. Panic took hold and everyone was running, Yago included, running through the water, an absurd slo-mo parody of actual running.

At first the herd had no direction, it darted and circled like a flock of startled birds, then headed toward the nearest of the low islands.

Hwang kept shouting, complaining, yelling, though Yago could see that whatever had grabbed his arm had let go now.

"My leg!" someone screamed.

Yago splashed, digging his arms in to propel himself forward, taking giant moon-gravity steps. His leading foot landed on nothing and he plunged face-down into the water. He sank beneath the surface. Claustrophobia shot syringes of adrenalin into his bloodstream and his brain began to slip gears, catching, slipping again.

No air, no air, no air. His eyes were open, blind, nothing but brown silt, swirling mud, choking him.

Then he felt it, the slide of flesh over flesh, the slimy touch of it across his belly. He slashed with the boomerang and came within an inch of gutting himself.

Yago screamed into the water and kicked against nothing.

Something grabbed his arm and pulled. He broke the surface, gasped, and tried to shake loose D-Caf's grip.

"Let go of me, you moron!" he yelled. He lowered his legs and touched ground. The water was up to his chest, no more.

"You were kind of splashing a lot," D-Caf said, giving him a sideways look. He held up the boomerang. "I got this back. You must have dropped it."

"One of those things attacked me," Yago said.

D-Caf held out the boomerang, ready to surrender it again.

"Keep it," Yago said. No way he could act as if the blade meant something. No way he could put himself any more in D-Caf's debt.

Rather than risk hitting another hole, Yago leaned into a swim. He was a strong swimmer, though only on the surface — not underwater, and he was soon well ahead of D-Caf.

The little twitch had seen him panic. Okay, everyone was panicking, but D-Caf had been calm and he'd seen that Yago was not. That was bad. No one could know about the claustrophobia. It was a glaring weakness. Someone would use it. Maybe even D-Caf himself. He was a twitch, but he was also the one who'd shot one of the Mayflower pilots. If you'd do that, you'd lock someone in a box without a second thought, lock them in a closet with no light and no handle on the door, bury them alive in a casket and . . .

"Get a grip, Yago," he told himself. "Get a grip. You're Yago. You're *Yago,* man."

Yago went through his ego mantra: Yago was the First Son. Son of the first African-American female president. He held undisputed title to "hottest teen" in America. The world. Everyone loved him, or else feared him. How many letters from how many girls? Hundreds of thousands. Millions. I want a picture, a lock of hair, a worn T-shirt, to see you, kiss you.

He'd been on the cover of just about every magazine. *Teen People* had named him "Sexiest Teen Alive." *The New York Times Magazine* had called him the "Brat in Chief." When he'd changed his hair to spring green, half the kids in the country had followed suit. When he'd had the cat-DNA eye treatment it had suddenly become one of the most common cosmetic procedures.

He was Yago, after all. Even here, even with no White House, no magazines, no fans, no letters, no . . . He was still Yago.

The mantra calmed him. The claustrophobia terror had replaced the fear of whatever was in the water. And now, with the suffocation fear receding he could see the other fear more objectively. The herd was still in full flight, wallowing heavily toward the island. Jobs and his little gaggle were vectoring in, too, the fear having proven contagious.

Yago slowed his pace. You didn't want to be the last person out of the water but, he sensed, you also didn't want to be the first person to step on that island.

He bobbed high, looking for Tamara Hoyle. She

was moving at a leisurely pace, carrying the baby high up on one shoulder. She wasn't worried about whatever was in the water. And she was in no hurry to reach the island. In fact, she was slowing down.

Yago stopped dead. He tread water till he realized he was now in shallows, less than waist high.

Yago's instinct for survival was ringing a big, loud bell. Tamara knew something. He didn't know how, but she knew something more than any of the rest of them did. Her and that mutant, eyeless freak of a baby.

He was a hundred feet from the island's edge. The sun was coming up behind it but the mist still seeped through the strange trees and alternately revealed and concealed.

Wylson and Burroway and Tate reached the island at about the same moment. They climbed, soggily, up onto the shore and immediately came the earsplitting metallic shriek of a Rider.

Two of the alien monsters appeared, stomping on foot through the mist. They stood there, staring balefully down at the humans with their face full of insect eyes.

Wylson raised her hands as if in surrender. "We don't want to fight, we don't want to fight," she practically sobbed.

The humans still in the water froze. Even Tamara was stock-still, waiting, watching. She seemed to feel Yago's eyes on her and turned to glare at him.

Suddenly, a sharp pain on the back of his thigh. He flailed, reached around, and touched something slime-coated and powerful.

It had him.